Always September

A novel by Doug Treat

Cover Design by Morgan Treat

1

For my wife, Amber, a true lover of books,
who encouraged me as I began to pursue writing
as my next adventure.

Chapter 1

Journal entry: "September 4th 2016 - 4:00 A.M. Well this is it! Should be hunting by tomorrow morning." Ethan wanted to write more in his journal, but he was in a hurry. He checked his packing list for backpacking/bow hunting again, but he knew he was good. He had already unpacked and re-packed his backpack four times yesterday to make sure he had everything he needed for the ten day backpacking trip he had planned.

He locked up the two thousand square foot "cabin" in northeastern Grand County, Colorado and jumped into the Lexus SUV. He had inherited the vacation house and vehicle after his parents had passed away. The Lexus was twelve years old, but still somehow smelled new. Ethan's dad had bought it just to keep in the garage for a vacation vehicle, but it still had less than five thousand miles on it.

He was in a hurry to get into Rocky Mountain National Park before anyone was out and about. He had a park pass, but it wasn't in his name. He knew that, at times, the park personnel at the Kawuneeche entrance kiosk would ask for ID and he could get turned back if he didn't get into the park before the employees were there.

Nobody was at the kiosk, so he drove through the gate and several miles into the park until his headlights hit the sign for the Bowen-Baker trailhead. There were two other vehicles in the dirt lot, both with overnight passes on the dash. Ethan clicked on his headlamp, pulled out his backpack, and looked to the northwest of the trailhead.

He found what he was looking for, a thick clump of willows where he could hide his pack until he could return. That done, he glanced about nervously. Even though it was still dark and the Bowen-Baker trailhead was not used heavily, it was still risky. His planning and caution paid off and he was able to drive slowly out of the park back toward his house near Grand Lake without drawing attention to himself.

Just south of the entrance station, he slowed and nearly stopped as he looked over at the visitor center parking lot on his left. He noted a ponderosa pine in the South part of the lot that had a scorched limb just above one of the parking spaces. Emotion overcame him and his breath caught in his throat.

His thoughts raced, imagining the event that had caused the burn just months prior. Ethan wasn't there, but still, he felt somewhat responsible and guilty for what had happened.

The sun was just lighting up the sky to the east when Ethan pulled the Lexus back into the garage and walked into the kitchen. Heart rate lessening now, he started making his breakfast and his nerves slowly started to calm down. He hadn't expected to be so nervous about the trip to cache his pack. Even now, several months after that fateful night at the visitor's center, his nerves were still shot. "I need to get out in the woods with a bow in my hand and an elk tag in my pocket," he thought. "Then, I can relax."

Sleeping most of the afternoon, Ethan woke refreshed and less stressed about the trip that would start tonight after it got dark.

He pulled out his wallet and dropped some of its contents on the kitchen counter to look at them again. One was his driver's license and the other, an archery elk hunting tag. Normally, not a cause for concern, he noted the different names on the two documents and vowed not to get caught, especially by the rangers in Rocky. They all knew the name on this hunting license and he would be in trouble if any of them saw the tag.

The trailhead to his hunting area started in Rocky Mountain National Park, but he would be hunting in a wilderness area just west of the Park. He considered leaving the elk tag behind, but it just didn't feel right to hunt without it, so he put both back in the wallet.

Ethan took a long, hot shower and shaved his face and neck before donning his lightweight camo hunting clothes. He then fixed a big steak and baked potato he had gotten for the occasion. He knew that another good meal and a shower were not in his immediate future, but he was still excited to get into the woods.

This valley now held some very painful memories and he needed a change of scenery. Sleeping in a tent and eating backpacking meals for a week and a half would be a small price to pay for the peace in his soul he was hoping this trip would provide.

He took his dinner into the game room to eat it while admiring the big bull elk above the fireplace mantle. The bull was about seven years old when he was taken and probably wouldn't have survived the upcoming winter. Seven years old is the elk equivalent of a great-great grandpa; one foot in the grave.

Ethan believed it was honoring to the animal to display this tribute to him above the fireplace. The taxidermy work was good and the bull looked like he had just stepped through the wall and was ready to let out a bugle. His essence would live long here, but he would have been scavenged by coyotes and bears if he had died in the woods, maybe even torn apart by the predators before he was dead.

Ethan knew that a single arrow had brought down the big bull in just a few minutes, a much better way to die than what nature typically provides. Admiring this elk awakened his excitement for the upcoming hunt. He was antsy to get going, but he had to wait another hour before he left so that it would be dark enough to not be noticed.

The moon was up and waxing crescent when Ethan made sure the house alarm was set, locked the door, and started on a fast walk back toward the trailhead where he had stashed his pack. He used the roads, but he had to dive into the ditch when cars would approach. Fortunately, the vehicle traffic was light that night, so he made good time, but still, the nine miles to the trailhead took nearly three hours.

He was relieved to find his pack as he had left it and felt inside to make sure the takedown recurve was still there. His quiver and arrows were strapped to the outside of the backpack and he flipped on his headlamp for just a few seconds to assure himself that no little critters had chewed on the feather fletchings. Chiding himself for taking the risk of using the light, he vowed to keep it off until well into the trees on the other side of the big valley.

He wrestled himself into his pack and pulled back his left sleeve to look at his watch. The luminescent hands of his analog watch said just after 1:00 A.M. when he started up the trail from the parking lot.

His pace slowed on the trail as he made his way across the Kawuneeche Valley or "*Valley of the Coyote*" in Arapahoe. It had been a long night already and his pack weight collaborated with the poor light to impede his progress. Ethan knew that he should have time to get into a safe camp in the forest to the west before the sun came up, so he took the hike slowly. He thought about the coyotes that the valley was named after, but he wasn't worried about them or even bears or mountain lions. The predators could see in the dark better than he could and would steer clear of the trail.

He just had to make sure that he didn't meet any people. He worried again about the conflicting documents in his wallet, but decided that the peace and solitude he expected on this hunt was worth the risk.

At the trail junction on the west side of the valley, a sliver of moonlight slid through the trees and dimly illuminated a trail sign to help him confirm that the left fork was the Bowen part of the trail, not that he needed the confirmation. He had spent countless hours studying the map in preparation for this trip over the last several weeks since he had broken into a neighboring cabin and found the bow, arrows, and elk license. Well, he hadn't really broken in. He knew that the door was never locked. "He won't mind if I use these," Ethan thought when he had taken the items.

It was 4:00 a.m. when he finally found a temporary campsite a mile off the trail and climbed into his sleeping bag, exhausted. He hadn't bothered to set up a tent since he would most likely find a more suitable camp site when he could see better tomorrow.

The smells of the forest quickly had him dreaming of chasing the majestic elk instead of the recurring nightmares that had plagued him for months back at the house. Four hours later, a smile stole across his face even before his eyes opened. He had awakened to the ethereal sound of a distant bugle, the mating call of the Rocky Mountain elk. "And so, it begins," he whispered to himself as he got up and assembled the custom takedown bow.

Chapter 2

Journal entry: "September 10, 2016-Never Summer Wilderness. Day six of the hunt. Finally feels like I'm a part of the woods now. Wish I could use calls, but don't want to call in another hunter. Been sitting at a wallow. Built a blind from fir and spruce branches seven yards from the wallow. Nearly happened last evening, but the wind switched at the last minute and they took off. Looked like four cows and a bull. So close."

Ethan was back in the blind writing in his journal after five hours of sitting. He was starting to get restless, but knew that he should stay until last light. Sure enough, just before dark he heard the soft mew of a cow elk as the evening light started to fade. Two elk, both cows, walked right into the middle of the pond and started to drink.

Ethan waited a few seconds to make sure they were settled down before starting to draw the recurve. The blind was slightly uphill from the water and was downwind from it for most of the day, but the evening thermal winds were cooling and starting to switch direction. He noticed a slight breeze on the back of his neck and one of the elk quickly raised her dripping nose high in the air to get a better smell. She didn't like what she smelled and started acting nervous, but the arrow was off before the elk had time to bolt for safety.

He had picked the closer cow who was quartering slightly away. He watched as the brightly colored fletching nearly disappeared into the spot he was aiming at just behind the shoulder. As the two elk exploded from the wallow, they kicked up water and mud, splattering Ethan in the face and arm. He noticed, as the target cow spun, that the sharp two-blade Zwickey broadhead had made it to the opposite side of the big animal. He knew the elk couldn't go far.

The trees were thick around the wallow, so he followed the elk with his ears as they ran downhill, breaking branches for several seconds; then all was quiet. Less than a minute later, a crash, and then he could hear what sounded like one animal continuing its flight down the hill.

"Bet it was less than forty yards," Ethan whispered to himself. He always tried to guess the recovery distance based on shot placement and how an animal reacted at the shot as a way of sharpening his outdoor skills.

As he waited his customary forty minutes, Ethan looked admiringly at the custom Bighorn recurve in his hands and read again the words written on the side of the riser, "*Custom Bighorn for Peter Blake.*" The side of the lower limb read *62" 52# @31.*" Since Ethan's draw length was twenty-eight inches, he drew about forty-seven pounds of draw weight with the bow.

He knew that most modern hunters considered that draw weight too light for elk, but he also knew that the heavy six hundred and thirty grain arrows didn't need a lot of speed to carry plenty of momentum.

He remembered what an old bowhunter had told him years ago. "The weight of the bow is not as important as the weight of the arrow. The best bow can't kill anything, so make sure you have the best arrows for the job."

As it turned out, the elk had made it fifty-five yards from the water hole and Ethan knew she had died in less than a minute from the shot. The fact that the elk had stopped after her initial sprint spoke to her lack of pain from the arrow. He was thankful to have made such an ethical shot. The sharp broadhead had caused a quick, nearly painless death, and the elk had passed out before she really knew she was in trouble.

He had to quarter the elk by headlamp. It was midnight before he got all the meat back to camp and hung up, protected from flies with some cotton pillowcases brought along for that purpose. His muscles ached from the work, but it was a good ache. Having sore muscles from the hard work after a successful hunt was part of the reward. Just before he drifted off to sleep, an idea came to him. It was a radical idea and one that required much further thought, but that would have to wait until tomorrow. Tonight he needed his sleep.

Chapter 3

Several months earlier:

Jacob Blake was alone with his thoughts as he sat on the side of his bed. He lived alone in a small cabin in the Colorado mountains, a place where he had been forced to move to as a teen, but now had grown to love.

Journal entry: "June 24, 2016-Looks like a good day for a new start. Cold this morning, but supposed to be a high of seventy-five." Jake took thirty minutes to write down his thoughts in his journal this cool summer morning. When he finished, he closed the leather book and let his finger trace the embossed letters of the lower right side of the cover "To Jacob. Love, M."

He wondered at the sudden rush of emotion that he felt, but was grateful for the recently unfamiliar feeling of feeling. It had been a while since he had experienced any emotion at all and this sadness was a welcome change from the familiar apathy of Jake's recent past.

Jake allowed a memory of when he had first made an entry in this journal. Well actually, it was a different notebook insert, but the same leather cover, now worn from years of use, but even more well-loved. It was fourteen years ago and he had just met her a few months earlier. They were both in the eighth grade and he was an angry teenager. She was the only classmate who understood him or…more accurately, he thought now, she was the only one who tried to; the only one who had made the effort.

The journal had been a Secret Santa gift given right before Christmas break when Jake's was in his first year at East Grand Middle School. At the time, Jake had thought that this Secret Santa gift giving thing was a joke, something you do in grade school, but not in eighth grade! "What a hick town!" he had said to one of the other boys on the bus ride home after the teacher had introduced the activity.

They had drawn names from one of the student's cowboy hat, of all things. The boy on the bus just nodded, but didn't say anything and quickly looked out the window at the falling snow. From the boy's reaction, Jake guessed that this class had been doing Secret Santa gifts since they were in grade school and maybe the other boy still enjoyed it. "What a hick town," he thought again, but this time, he didn't voice what he was thinking.

The following week in school, his classmates had exchanged gifts. When he had opened the journal, he felt a tinge of regret for what he had given to Sarah, the girl he had drawn. He had seen her disappointment as she unwrapped the *Kit Kat* candy bar he bought at the convenience store in Grand Lake Village just that morning. Maybe he should have put more thought into his gift.

It had taken a minute for Jake to realize the identity of his Secret Santa who had given the much-nicer-than-a-candy-bar gift. There was only a "To Jake" on the outside of the package, but when his eyes finally spotted the "Love M" on the cover of the journal he could feel the heat rush to his cheeks as his eyes searched the room for her. Molly was staring at him from across the room. He noticed her just holding her wrapped gift on her lap as all the kids around were ripping into theirs.

Jake mouthed a silent thank you to her and Molly's face exploded into a smile. Now, years later, he knew that's when he had fallen for her, that first time she smiled at him. Her quick smile, especially how her eyes lit up, did something to Jake that he couldn't understand back then. It was the single most attractive part of Molly for Jake. The rest of her was not hard to look at, but there was that smile! Molly's smile could always wreck him.

Going back in his memory further, Jake recalled when he had first talked to Molly Baker. She had asked if she could sit by him in the cafeteria. It was the Tuesday after Labor Day that first school year in Grand County. During that first lunch together, Jake had surprised himself and had told her some, but not all of his story, just because she went out of her way to be nice to him.

Most of the other kids avoided him. He was weird and a loner, with a quick temper. Jake was not big, but he had proven to be strong and quick. Whenever another guy thought it might be fun to try to fight him, which only happened twice that year, everybody in school learned it wasn't a good idea. His quickness had ended the fights within seconds.

Jake had told Molly that both his parents had died almost exactly a year ago and he was now living with his Uncle Peter in his cabin northwest of Grand Lake.

"Oh, is that by the Grand Lake Lodge?" she asked. "I love that old place." Jake had not been there, but Uncle Peter had pointed out the sign one day when they were on their way to Rocky Mountain National Park.

"No," Jake had responded. "Well, yeah. I guess it's close. I don't know," he stumbled.

Molly told him that it was a tradition for her parents and her to go to the lodge for dinner on her birthday, which was September 3rd. Since she was six, she had always said "Grand Lake Lodge!" when her parents asked her where she wanted to go for her birthday meal.

After Jake received his journal, he remembered what Molly had said about the lodge. He wanted to get her a Christmas present too, so he rode his bicycle there the following Saturday. He took a picture of the front of the lodge with the *Polaroid* his parents had given him for his twelfth birthday. He then cut some aspen branches with his uncle's saw he had brought along for that purpose.

Back at the cabin, Uncle Peter showed him how to use his "arm-powered miter saw," as he liked to call it, but Jake dubbed it the slowest saw in the world. He had cut the pieces with the hand saw and assembled his aspen branch picture frame for the *Polaroid* photo of the lodge.

Uncle Peter wisely didn't ask who the frame and picture were for, but he accurately guessed that there might be a girl involved. He was just happy that his new charge wasn't moping around the cabin so much these days and was hopefully finally making some friends; not that Peter Blake knew much about friends...or girls for that matter.

He had loved a girl once, back in Nebraska, but that was a long time ago and he made it a point not to think too much about that. He was too old now and liked his life as a hermit. The boy was growing on him though.

"There's hope for this generation yet," he thought, referring to his nephew, his brother's son. "Think he might turn out all right, in spite of his grumpy old uncle."

For Jake, at twenty-nine years old now, these early memories of life in Grand County, Colorado, were at once, both sweet and painful. Uncle Peter was now buried out back behind the cabin. Well, his ashes were.

Jake still lived in the old cabin. Uncle Peter left him all his earthly possessions in his will, a surprise to Jake. It made sense because there were no other living family members, but it was still unexpected.

Jake hadn't realized that he had closed his eyes while all these memories came flooding back, nor that he was clutching his journal to his chest so tightly that his knuckles were white. He wondered if the tears streaming down his cheeks were for his uncle or for Molly.

He had lost his uncle several years ago, and now it appeared, he may have lost Molly.

Jake wiped the tears from the leather cover and fingered again the words embossed there…"Jacob." Only she called him that. She always had. Everyone else, he had corrected. "It's Jake," he would say sternly, "just Jake."

Even though it sounded funny to say Jake Blake, he preferred the name Jake. With her though, he never corrected. From the very first time, it somehow just felt right for Molly to call him Jacob. He wanted a special name for her too, so he started to simply call her "M" for the first letter of her name. It stuck.

Jake placed his journal carefully, even reverently, on the bookshelf in the cabin and glanced at his watch, "7:45." He was going to have to hurry to get a run in before his appointment at 9:00 in Granby.

Running east along the main road from Uncle Peter's cabin (it still didn't feel right to think of the cabin as his own), he was surprised to see the familiar blue and white Grand County ambulance pulling out of the driveway of the big log house, a quarter mile east of his uncle's.

"I thought nobody lived there," he thought as he jogged closer. The house wasn't visible from the road. The high fence, high-tech security cameras and alarms, and keypad entry gate kept most people from ever seeing the house.

Jake's friend from school, Mike Anderson, had given him a tour of the house several years ago when he was remodeling the kitchen. Mike had worked for Baker Construction, Molly's dad, as a carpenter since high school.

"$150 K remodel, just the kitchen," Mike had said, "and nobody lives here. The owners used to come out for several weeks every summer, but nobody's been here for years. This project must be a tax write-off or something."

The ambulance drove slowly toward town and Jake noted that the lights were on inside the patient compartment, indicating that they were transporting a patient, but no lights and sirens.

"Non-emergent," he thought as he ran. "Must not be too serious."

Several years ago, Jake had done several ride-alongs with Grand County EMS. He knew most of the EMTs and medics, some of them from high school, but they all avoided him now when he ran into them in Granby or Grand Lake.

Jake had grown to love small town living where everybody knows everybody else but now…now that he had screwed up, well…now it was different.

Folks in a small tight-knit community will defend each other fiercely, but once you cross that invisible line; once you mess things up badly enough, forgiveness and acceptance is nearly impossible to regain.

This place was small enough that you can't just move to the next town. The whole county knows when you mess up.

Jake sighed audibly and finished his run just in time to shower and change into some nice jeans and a pullover fleece over his T-shirt. "Probably too hot for the fleece later in the day," he thought, but he could keep it on until after his meeting in town, just to look a bit more presentable.

His fully restored, bright red 1974 Toyota Land Cruiser kicked up a few rocks as Jake gunned it around a corner on the gravel road towards town. His pride and joy, at least he still had the Cruiser, a small consolation for how the rest of his life was going right now.

Chapter 4

Molly welcomed the interruption to her morning to get out of the hospital for a moment. She had to drive to City Market Pharmacy to fill a prescription for one of the hospital floor patients.

The small mountain hospital didn't have much of a pharmacy in-house. It seemed inefficient for the charge nurse to be doing a pharmacy run, but it came with the territory at Middle Park Health. They were often short-staffed and after she got all the nursing staff going for the day, she was actually the most expendable, the rest of the nurses busy with patient care.

Molly metaphorically took off her charge nurse hat and donned the gopher hat to "go for" whatever was needed. While she had the hat on, she decided to pick up coffee and some pastries for the staff on the way back, which she did often.

Her considerate and kind nature, combined with her medical competence made her a favorite with patients and staff alike. Both baristas at the local coffee shop smiled broadly when they saw Molly come through the door. She was a favorite all over Grand County for her simple beauty, both inside and out.

Molly had done well in nursing school, but she was surprised how quickly she was assigned as a charge nurse at the hospital. It was probably due more to the high nurse turnover rate in the small mountain hospital rather than her own talents. Still, she was both humbled and proud of her success here in just a few short years.

"Humble and proud?" she thought to herself as she struggled to get her keys out while balancing the coffee and pastries on her way back to her car. "Not sure if that's possible. Will have to consult the journal." She smiled. She always got more clarity with her thoughts after writing them down in her journal.

After she gave Jacob his journal back in the eighth grade, she told him that it helped her sort out her thoughts to write them down. Jake noticed that it helped him too after he had been journaling for a month or so.

Molly never did tell him that she had traded Leah Miller for his name so that she could be his Secret Santa. She preferred that he think fate had brought them together, drawn out of some kid's cowboy hat.

Before she pulled out of the coffee shop parking lot, Molly saw it out of the corner of her eye and involuntarily caught her breath. It was hard to miss; that bright red Land Cruiser.

She loved that thing and hated it at the same time, perhaps another conundrum for her journal. She had loved riding in the cruiser when she was in high school and was known around town as Jake's co-pilot, being so often in the passenger seat.

She hated it on Junior prom night when she had ripped her dress trying to climb in. Jake had salvaged the evening by taking her to the spa at Hot Sulfur Springs instead after trading their formal attire for swimming gear.

Jacob had looked a bit silly in Molly's dad's borrowed swim trunks but…"Love is blind, I guess," she said now under her breath as the Toyota passed.

"Look away!" she silently yelled at herself, but she knew she couldn't. She caught a profile view of him with his black, curly, shoulder-length hair back in a ponytail like he used to wear it at work. She preferred it down and loved how crazy it was, sticking up all over, doing whatever it wanted. His hair behaved like its owner, just like it was that first time she saw him in the eighth grade.

She noticed that his beard was longer than normal and as wild and unkempt as his hair. Jacob was usually very fastidious about his beard. He trimmed it and brushed it religiously, adding beard oil.

"What was the name? Oh, yeah, *Jeremy's Beard Oil*." It smelled of aloe and lavender, but still was masculine somehow.

Jacob had started using *Jeremy's* as soon as he grew out his beard in high school. Most of the boys in high school had scruffy facial hair, but by the tenth grade, Jacob's beard was full and black like his hair.

As the Cruiser passed, Molly checked to make sure the specialized license plates were still there and was relieved to see "JKSJEEP" still firmly attached, a gift from her on his nineteenth birthday.

At first Jacob hated people calling his Toyota a "Jeep," but she had called it that once in jest, just because she knew that it would bug him. After that, it had become their own private joke. He had loved the gift and ten minutes after opening it, had the new plates swapped out for the old on the Cruiser.

Driving back to the hospital, Molly wondered what Jacob was doing in town today. It seemed strange that she couldn't just text and say "Hey. Saw the Jeep. Whatcha doin?" like she used to.

After parking at the hospital employee lot, Molly pulled out her phone and clicked on "Jacob." She stared at the last text from her which read, "Jacob, please STOP! Don't text again!" and he hadn't since…she looked at the date…March 4th, more than three months!

"Why do you do that, Molly? Why torture yourself by looking. He's not going to text," she yelled out loud at herself in the rearview mirror of her car. Her reflection didn't answer and she knew her journal wouldn't either.

Chapter 5

Jake was acutely aware of people noticing his Cruiser as he drove through the town of Granby. He used to like the attention and admiration that his vehicle brought him, but now he only felt judgment as people that he knew would stare, but not wave at the very recognizable 4x4 as he drove past.

He pulled up and parked beside a white mailbox reading "Williams" in front of a small blue house in need of some fresh paint.

Joan Williams had been a math teacher at Middle Park High School until she retired two years ago. Now, she ran Williams Employment Services part-time where she helped with job placement and limited financial help for small businesses in the area.

Jake knocked on the side door of the house that had been added as a business entrance and glanced up at a small sign reading "W.E.S." above the door. Everyone knew that the office was just a converted bedroom in the small house, but somehow, the separate entrance made the business seem more legitimate. WES was also a tribute to Wes Williams, Joan's late husband.

The gray haired lady in her late sixties seemed just as lively and cheerful as she was when she was Jake's teacher in high school.

"Hi, Mrs. Williams," Jake said as she ushered him into her office.

"Please, Jake. Call me Joan. Having adults call me Mrs. Williams makes me feel old."

"Okay, Joan," he said, but it didn't sound quite right. "Have you found any jobs for me that might work?" Jake had called W. E. S. last week to ask about possible employment and Joan had texted him yesterday asking him to come in.

"Well, Jake," she started, her voice hinting a little bit of pessimism. "It's not been easy to find someone willing to give you a chance, especially after the...uh...incident."

Jake winced. He knew that "the incident" was what had happened last fall at the hometown high school football game. His mind quickly went back to that night while he waited for Mrs. Williams to find the papers she was looking for.

Normally, the Panthers do pretty well filling the seats for a Friday night game, but that night, the stands were especially full since the "Trail Ridge Trophy" was up for grabs in the game against the Estes Park Bobcats.

Jake had not been doing well for over a year. He hadn't yet admitted his addiction to narcotics, not even to himself, but by the time of "the incident," he was fully addicted. The day of the game had been especially hard on Jake as he had lost his dream job, it was the anniversary of his parents' deaths, and even his girlfriend Molly was on the verge of leaving him because he couldn't seem to control his drug use.

He had woken up that morning already in despair and had added alcohol to the narcotics all day. He hadn't felt the loss of his parents this hard since the year that they had died. He tried to numb the pain with the substance abuse, but nothing seemed to work.

He knew he should sleep it off, but in the afternoon he decided that maybe watching the local football game would remind him of happier times and pull him out of his slump. Amazingly, he had been able to drive to the football field without running into anything or driving off the road.

Jake didn't remember much about that night, but his friends told him later that he had snuck a large bottle of whisky into the game. He was completely wasted by halftime.

He had noticed a small group of his high school classmates gathered near the concession stand during the halftime break. Molly was in the group and they were laughing about something that they had remembered from their high school days.

In his stupor, Jake thought that they were laughing at him. He stumbled to his Cruiser, retrieved his service pistol from behind the seat, and started toward the group. Apparently, he had yelled some obscenities and loudly told the group to shut up and that he would rather be dead than to have people laugh at him. He then raised the handgun and fired it into the air, but he didn't remember any of it.

His action swiftly resulted in a better tackle than the spectators had yet seen that night by two Grand County deputies who were at the game. This was followed by a seventy-two hour mental health hold at a psych hospital in Denver.

The incident had caused the football game to be canceled, the only non-weather related cancellation in Panthers history. Known locally as "Jake's mistake," the incident had caused nearly as much of a stir in Grand County as when John Heemeyer had smashed several downtown buildings in Granby with his bulldozer in 2004.

After Jake was released from his mental health hold and had come back home, the whole incident worked to sober him up and highlighted the gravity of his addiction. Nobody was hurt, but they easily could have been.

Jake had been clean since that night, but even so, most people still didn't trust him and Molly had officially broken up with him the following week. Jake had tried for several months to make amends and get back together with her, but Molly had made it clear that she didn't trust him and didn't want to date anymore.

"I was able to find a few options," Joan continued. Jake's mind snapped back to the present. " But, I don't know if you'll like them very much compared to your park ranger job."

Jake knew that, for him, no job would compare to working for the Park, but he needed to show everyone, especially Molly, that he could hold down a job, any job.

"Okay. What you got?" he said, trying to sound more optimistic than he felt.

"Okay. So, here's one," Joan said, pushing a piece of paper across her desk toward Jake. He read the description for a loader at the feed store. "Must be able to lift and move heavy loads. Minimum wage. Forklift training for the right employee after six months." Jake wondered if a drug addict was the "right employee."

"Ok, that might work," Jake said, now sounding more pessimistic. "Anything else?"

"Just this security officer job," Joan stated as she handed him another paper. It was for Spencer Security. Joan explained that Don Spencer had moved into Grand County a few years back and had started the business.

"Normally, Mr. Spencer wouldn't be looking for someone in your...situation, but I vouched for your character and he's desperate to get new officers to some new security contracts that he just got. The position he needs to fill right away is a security position at the hospital. They actually want him to send someone tonight if possible."

"I'll take it!" Jake said without hesitation.

"Jake, are you sure?" Joan questioned. She knew that Jake, working at the hospital with his old girlfriend, would probably end up badly for both of them. Joan thought they were a cute couple in high school, but now, well, there was a lot of water under the bridge.

"Why don't you move away, out of the county? Go to where nobody knows you. Start fresh. I hear Fort Collins is nice." Jake thought for several seconds before answering. He knew that Mrs. Williams was right, but he also knew that he had to keep trying with Molly until he knew for sure that no hope was left.

"Nope…I'll take it." He sounded more confident than he felt, but decided that working at the hospital would give him the clarity he needed. He would rather know for sure if Molly still had feelings for him or if she really was over him. Then, he would know what to do next.

Jake and Joan worked out the details for the security job and Jake left with a "Thanks, Mrs. Williams" on his way out the door, forgetting her request to call her by her first name.

As soon as Jake left, Joan called Molly at the hospital. She wanted to give her a heads-up that Jake would be the new security officer starting tonight. Molly didn't sound very pleased on the phone, but had remained professional. Joan, while concerned, hoped for the best.

Chapter 6

Jake nervously looked at himself in the mirror again. After meeting his new boss and getting instructions about the new job, he was back home getting ready for work. He had trimmed up his beard and even found the beard oil that he hadn't used in months.

He thought through several different scenarios that could be played out tonight when Molly saw him. He was supposed to report to the nurse's station at 5:30 and he knew that Molly got off at 6:00, so there would be a little bit of overlap in their schedules.

Thinking maybe he should text to give her a warning that he was coming, he remembered her last text and decided against it. He knew he should eat dinner, but he was too nervous. He threw some *protein* bars and an apple in his backpack and jumped into the Cruiser.

Parking in the employee parking lot at the hospital, a lump caught in Jake's throat as he noticed Molly's car. He nearly lost his nerve and drove away, but instead, he forced himself to see this through no matter the outcome.

A part of him said to just forget it. It would be easier to not face her and to live with the illusion that she might come back instead of confirming that she definitely wouldn't and die inside. He knew that it would be painful if she totally rejected him; if she told him that there was no hope for a future for them, but in the end he would rather know the truth, no matter how painful the rejection could be.

Before the drugs had changed him, he had learned to live that way. He would live courageously again. She had actually taught him that.

Praying for more time to steel his nerves, his watch declined his request for more time with its "5:27" proclamation. He took a big breath and walked through the front doors of the hospital.

At the nurses station, Jake was relieved that there was another nurse there that he didn't recognize. She was a temp nurse named Hannah from Idaho who had only been working there for about ten weeks.

She definitely wasn't shy. He found out nearly everything about her after only a few minutes of conversation. Hannah was quite taken with this new security officer and was excited to introduce him to the job, and it seemed, even more excited to introduce him to herself.

Jake tried to focus on what she was saying, but kept looking around for Molly. Hannah was mid-sentence when Molly suddenly came out of a patient room causing Jake to catch his breath. Hannah noticed and turned around to see what he was staring at.

"Oh yeah, that's Molly. She's the charge nurse so…" Hannah's voice trailed off as she realized that Jake was no longer listening.

"Yes, we know each other from high school," Molly inserted. "Hello, Jacob. Welcome to the team. Okay Hannah, could you check in on room four? I'll fill in Mr. Blake before I get off my shift."

Reluctantly, Hannah gave up her self-appointed role as the orientation officer for new employees and returned to her nursing duties.

Molly continued in a low voice, almost a whisper, "Okay, this will have to be strictly professional, Jacob or you won't be here long. Do you understand?"

"Yes, ma'am!" he replied, smiling, but Molly did not return the smile. "Sorry, M. I know this is…"

Molly cut him off. "Call me Molly." She turned and continued his orientation for the job.

Jake tried to listen carefully as Molly explained hospital protocol and his role there specifically, but he was also trying to read her voice and behavior for any hint of the old familiarity; the old feelings between them. True to her word, Molly stayed completely professional and neutral towards Jake as she talked and showed him around.

Jake did catch that the patient in room three was his responsibility for the next three nights.

"He has some pre-existing medical conditions, but you need to be in the room all night since we have only one nurse on the floor for the graveyard, okay?"

"Got it."

Molly continued, "He's on a seventy-two hour hold because they found a suicide note in his house this morning."

"Fair enough."

"Any other questions?" At the shake of Jake's head, Molly grabbed her tote bag. "Ok, I'm done with my shift. If you need anything, just ask the other nursing staff." Molly quickly walked down the hall and around the corner and to her car before Jake could see the tears welling up in her eyes.

They were fifty feet apart and couldn't hear the other, but they both whispered, "This is going to be harder than I thought," at exactly the same time.

Chapter 7

Jake entered room three and glanced at his patient who was asleep. He was hooked up to a monitor and had an IV dripping into the crook of his left arm. Jake noticed the yellow hue to the patient's skin and wondered why he was jaundiced.

He took a look at the patient chart noting the name and birthday, "Ethan Wagner 2/13/87." He was just a few months older than Jake. The chart also told Jake that Ethan had chronic liver disease and that he had been found passed out this morning on the dirt road close to where Uncle Peter's cabin was.

Jake reasoned that Ethan must be the patient from the ambulance that he saw this morning. He noted that his mailing address was from Pennsylvania. At 1:00 A.M., Jake's patient was still sleeping and Jake was wondering how he could stay awake until 6:00 when he got off. He had been up since early yesterday morning since he hadn't planned on working this job. He realized now that he would be up for nearly twenty-four hours before he got to his bed to sleep again. He would have to adjust his sleep schedule in the future to make this work.

Molly had told him that they normally transfer psych patients to Denver, but mental health couldn't find any beds available. They had to keep this patient here for the seventy-two hour hold and then continue to manage his medical condition beyond that.

Jake's background as an EMT helped him to understand some of the medical side of this new job, but treating patients out in the field was quite different from this more controlled hospital setting. He wasn't entirely comfortable with it.

Jake's thoughts were interrupted with, "Are you my babysitter?"

"I guess so," he replied, "I'm Jake."

Ethan managed a weak smile and a "pleasure to make your acquaintance," stated with excessive formality for the situation.

Jake decided to broach the subject right away to clear the air. He hoped that his patient would appreciate frankness and up-front honesty. "So, they tell me that you wanted to kill yourself. What's the story with that?"

Ethan sat up a little in bed and managed another smile, wider this time.

"How much time have you got?"

"Well, as it turns out, I will be your um…'babysitter' for the entire seventy-two hours, at least at night."

"Well then, I will attempt to sleep during the day and keep you awake at night telling you my story. I've already figured out that it's best to fake sleep when that nurse, Hannah, comes in to take vitals anyway. She'll talk your ear off!"

They both laughed at their shared first impressions of Hannah. They both felt a bond and immediate trust with the other.

Ethan decided to start back in his childhood to draw out the story and give them something to talk about for the full three nights. "I am an only child from Pennsylvania…" he began.

Chapter 8

Jake learned that, although Ethan was raised in a wealthy family, his childhood was less than idyllic.

"My dad owned a successful insurance company in Philadelphia. He built up the company from just a few brokers when he was in his twenties to now, it has over three dozen. By his forties, my dad no longer had to go into the office anymore."

Ethan allowed a slight smile as he added, "Dad never did anything halfway. In college he started shooting competitive Olympic style archery. He even made it on to the US Olympic team before I was born, but by then his business took all of his time and he was not able to practice with his bow enough to stay at the top of his game.

"I was five the first time I remember seeing him shoot. He took me to a 3-D competition and I watched as he loosed shot after shot without a miss. At that young age, I was surprised that other shooters were sometimes shooting eights or fives, but my dad only scored tens and twelves for the entire competition.

"He made it look easy with his recurve while other shooters were struggling to stay on target, even with compound bows. He was incredibly focused and calm when he shot and he taught me to shoot as well, focusing all of my childhood energy into the shot.

"By the time I was ten, I was winning most of my archery competitions, both 3-D and paper targets. By twelve, I was getting bored with stationary targets, so Dad and I started hunting with our traditional bows, first for whitetail and turkeys in Pennsylvania and then we started hunting all over.

"When I was really young, mom used to come to watch us compete and she even came on some of our hunting trips, turning them into a shopping and spa vacation for her, but I never saw her shoot.

"Dad told me that she was really good in college. That's how they met. They shot a lot together when they first started dating, but after I was born, mom struggled with anxiety and depression.

"I don't remember too many times when she was truly happy. She could fake it well at dinner parties and charity events, but Dad and I knew that it was only a facade.

"I remember one party where she had fooled everyone into thinking that she was the happiest person in the room, but when we got home, she immediately started drinking and didn't sober up for a week.

"It was like she became addicted to her depression. She would sometimes come out of it for a while and she would enjoy something, but then she would get uncomfortable, like she didn't feel like she was supposed to be happy. She seemed to feel more at home with the familiar feelings of anxiety and depression and she would feel uncomfortable when she was content and at peace.

"I remember once, I must have been about seven, I was laughing at a TV show that I was watching. She came into the room and told me to turn it off; that my laughter was giving her a headache.

"I wish I would have known her before or…I wish she would have died before I had a memory of her. The only mom I ever knew was already dead, she just forgot to stop breathing."

Jake interjected, "Sorry, man. That really sucks." He remembered fondly his relationship with his own mother and was grateful that his memories of her were mostly good memories.

Ethan continued the story of how his dad bought the property in Grand County to try to pull Ethan's mom out of her funk; a place where they could come to unwind and get away from Philly for a while and let nature do her calming work.

Sometimes, Ethan's mom would get better for a few days when they would come to Colorado, but then she would drop back into her familiar pattern of anxiety and despair. She would inevitably cut the vacation short and demand to go home where her bottles of pills and alcohol were her most trusted friends.

When Ethan was thirteen, his dad got Colorado archery elk tags for both of them, hoping that his wife would also want to come along and stay at the cabin.

"Dad got a nice bull with his recurve that trip. The mount is hanging in the cabin, but we didn't have much fun. Mom refused to come and we knew that she would be worse than ever being left at home alone.

"You know, I didn't really care if Mom wanted to destroy her life, but it was really difficult to see how hard Dad tried to make her happy. I saw how much it hurt him to see her ignore his attempts to try to help her get emotionally and mentally healthy.

"As a kid, I couldn't understand why Dad's efforts weren't working. I thought he was doing something wrong, but now I see that if a person doesn't have any self-respect or self-worth, nobody else can externally make someone love themself.

"Dad also turned to alcohol to numb his pain of losing mom. She physically was still there, but she was gone emotionally and it was as if Dad himself was dying; bleeding out from a thousand small cuts.

"I grew to expect nothing from Mom as she became more and more distant from us. Then 9/11 happened!"

"Wait, what?! What do you mean?" Jake had been listening intently to Ethan's story, but now his ears were burning. His own history was so tied up with the events of 9/11/2001 and he caught his breath as some of the memories of that day came flooding back. It was amazing enough to find someone else who was into traditional archery like he was, especially here in a hospital room, but Jake was astounded to think that they both also may have something in common with 9/11!

Chapter 9

Jake was literally on the edge of his chair when Ethan mentioned 9/11 and he waited patiently for him to continue, but he was going to have to wait a bit longer for the rest of the story.

It was 3:00 a.m. and Ethan was too tired and weak to continue tonight. He promised Jake that they would talk again and he would continue his story the following night.

As Ethan slept, Jake studied his face. He reflected on how ironic it was that someone like Ethan, born into wealth in Pennsylvania, could be here in Colorado, dying of liver disease and wanting to end his own life.

Jake compared himself to Ethan. His family was never wealthy, but in some ways, it sounded like his childhood experience might have been richer than Ethan's; his upbringing had been more abundant in love and acceptance. But, like Ethan, he had also been on the verge of despair many times.

He was now. It seemed his whole existence was wrapped up in the forgiveness or rejection of Molly. He couldn't imagine her forgiving him for what he had allowed himself to become, but he also couldn't imagine living his life without her.

These thoughts, and darker ones that threatened to overwhelm, occupied his time until the morning charge nurse came in to tell him that they now had enough staff to keep an eye on his patient and he was free to go.

On the drive home, Jake reflected on what had happened that night. Ethan's story and Molly's coldness toward Jake had put him in a contemplative, depressed mood and he wondered if he would be able to sleep when he got home. As soon as his head hit the pillow, however, the last eventful day and the mental toll of wondering how Molly would respond to him combined to propel him into a deep sleep.

Jake woke himself up seven hours later yelling out, "No!" In his groggy state, he struggled to remember his dream and what he had been yelling about.

In a few minutes, he recalled that he was dreaming about his former job as a park ranger. He was on the trail to Adam's Falls in Rocky and he was running up the trail. He remembered that dispatch was repeating "Hurry! Hurry! Hurry!" on his radio. He could hear the roar of the falls before he could see them, so in his dream, he knew that it must have been late spring or early summer when snowmelt was at its height.

As the falls came into view, he noticed a crowd of people standing on the rocks about halfway down the falls. All of them had their eyes fixed to the top of the falls where a solitary figure was standing right on the edge of the river. One slip would take him down the falls and, with this kind of flow, to a sure death.

His boots felt like lead as he tried to run up the rocks to where the man stood facing the river. As he approached, he noticed that the man was wearing a park uniform and he wondered which one of his co-workers would put themselves in such a precarious position.

Somehow, over the noise of the roaring river, he heard the crowd all start to chant, "jump, jump, jump…" Astonished at their cruelty, he held out a hand indicating for them to stop and, as he did, he noticed they were all people that he knew from Grand Lake and Granby.

He realized finally that the man was suicidal and was ready to jump into the falls. "Wait! Don't do this!" he yelled, but the man seemed to only hear the yells of the crowd. With one leap he thrust himself into the top of the falls. He twisted so that he was face up just before he hit the water.

Jake rushed to where the man had been standing, but he was unable to reach him and he was lost under the turbulent water. The man's park uniform hat had flown off just before he hit the water. "No!" he heard himself yell as he awoke.

Usually Jake had trouble remembering his dreams, but this one he recalled in vivid detail and he awoke with a strong feeling of despair and fear. He thought he should journal about it, but he first needed to clear his mind with a run.

The June sunshine felt good as he stepped out of the door. It felt strange to run in the early afternoon since he normally would go for a run in the morning, but he was determined to try to keep his normal routine as much as possible even with this new work schedule.

Normally, running would totally clear Jake's thoughts. It worked almost like a mental reset button for him. Today though, he couldn't shake the thoughts and feelings of his dream. Halfway through the two mile run, he suddenly stopped and gasped as he remembered details of the last few moments of his dream.

As the man was falling into the roaring river, he twisted his body to look at the crowd and Jake could hear him whisper, "she didn't come," even over the roar of the river. He now remembered the sad face just before it plunged into the icy water–his own face!

Chapter 10

Ethan had been able to sleep well during the day and felt rested when Jake returned for his shift. Both men were anxious to continue the story and both were finding connection through the telling.

It had been cathartic for Ethan to tell his story to someone who would just listen and not try to fix something. Ethan had seen many counselors and mental health professionals over the years for depression and alcohol abuse, but he couldn't recall anyone ever listening to his whole story without stopping him to offer advice or to try to correct him.

When Jake walked in, Ethan noticed right away that he was agitated about something. "What's up?"

"Oh...I'm good," Jake lied. "Just a weird dream and..." he hesitated, not sure how much to share with his new friend, "...a girl," he finished weakly.

Molly had just given him a few instructions before she left at the end of her shift. She had been professional, but terse with Jake.

"Ah, there's always a girl, huh? I have one of those stories myself."

"Speaking of stories," Jake interjected, glad to find an excuse not to talk about his present troubles. "What's up with your story and 9/11?"

Ethan sighed as the memories of that time came flooding back. "My mom was already anxious and depressed, but when 9/11 happened, her mental and emotional health problems really escalated. She became obsessed with the news of what was happening in New

York. She watched and rewatched the footage of the Twin Towers, the planes as they crashed into them, the people jumping, everything.

"She was often confused about the story too, at times thinking that it had happened in Philadelphia. One time, she told me a story that her dad had been in the plane and had tried to stop the hijackers. Grandpa had been gone for seven years. She said that they had slit his throat, but he had still managed to find a parachute for a little boy who made it safely off the plane before it hit the building. 'That little boy was Ethan', she had said, forgetting that she was talking to me.

"Her drinking and drug abuse became way worse, adding to her paranoia and mental decline. She refused to leave the house, so Dad hired psychologists and substance abuse specialists to work with her at home.

"She was verbally very abusive to anyone new who came in, so none of them lasted too long on the job. She didn't trust anyone and thought they were all terrorists, even Dad sometimes. I was the only one that she was always okay with, even when she was at her worst. She would often say that we have to stick together and that nobody else could be trusted.

"For a year, Dad never left the house and he wanted me there as much as possible to calm her down. School was my only reprieve, but Dad didn't want me to play sports or hang out with my friends. I couldn't be away for long or Mom would flip out. I found myself almost as depressed as mom.

"Dad had always been a heavy drinker, but he really got serious about it then. Being stuck at home, Dad and I weren't able to bond over archery or hunting. We bonded over alcohol and I was drinking way more than any kid needs to be drinking.

"Summers were especially bad because I couldn't escape the house to go to school. The summer of '02, I begged dad to let me go to a two-week camp that some of my friends were going to in July. Normally, I would prefer to just shoot my bow or go on a hunt or camping trip with my dad, but I could see that that wasn't in the cards that year, so I was desperate to do something where I could escape the chaos at home.

"I remember two things about the camp, the firefighters that came to talk to us with their big ladder truck and Tanya, a girl I met there. I fell for Tanya hard.

"When I got back home, things were bad for Mom and Dad, but better for me. I had two new distractions. I became obsessed with becoming a firefighter and obsessed with Tanya.

"When I wasn't busy trying to calm Mom down, I would spend hours studying about firefighting or writing letters to Tanya.

"Kids didn't have cell phones back then and Tanya's parents didn't want her on the home phone talking to this random guy from camp that they didn't know, so we wrote letters. I didn't want to scare her away, so I avoided any talk about my family, but I would tell her how rich we were and I sent pictures of our house or cars.

"She seemed to be very interested in how I lived. It was novel to her as she was from a lower income family. She lived in Harrisburg where her dad worked as a custodian at the Philadelphia Macaroni Company there.

"At first, when she told me where her dad worked, I thought it was a joke, but Tanya assured me that it was a real place that makes pasta. I guess I had never thought about where macaroni comes from.

"Never was I more excited for school to start than that year. Dad even gave me a longer leash since it seemed that Mom had been stable, or at least wasn't getting any worse. I tried out for football and got on the team, not as a starter, but at least I was on the team.

"I actually wasn't interested in playing, but it seemed to be the best way to extend my school time away from home. Sometimes, we would practice before and after school. Most of the kids hated 'two-a-days', but I loved it. Being away from home for most of my waking hours gave me a much needed break from my Mom.

"I remember that it was a Wednesday and we had two-a-day practices getting ready for a big game that Friday. In my mind, these workouts weren't just for football, but they were getting me in shape for being a firefighter.

"I didn't even realize it was 9/11, the first anniversary of the attacks, until we had a moment of silence in my English class. The teacher showed some pictures and footage of the attacks. I could see that a lot of the kids were very emotional when they saw the footage. I thought it was strange that they were so moved by it, because I was numb to it. It had been on every day at my house for a year.

"That night, after a hard practice, I got home at about 6:00 and I was starving. Dad stopped me from going to the kitchen and asked me to check in on Mom. He told me that she had been hysterical that morning, worse than he'd ever seen. In her delusional state, she thought that the news, recounting and observing 9/11, was reporting on another attack live.

"When he tried to reason with her, she accused him of being one of the terrorists and thought that she was on the plane. He realized that she wasn't going to calm down with him there, so he left her room and just listened at the door until she was quiet and he could just hear the TV.

"I could smell alcohol on Dad's breath and I felt sorry for him having to live like this. Then, I felt sorry for Mom, who was never able to relax and enjoy herself. Most of all, I felt sorry for myself. I shouldn't be the most put together person in this house. I was supposed to be the kid here.

"I vividly remember walking into Mom's TV room that day and feeling that something was terribly wrong. I couldn't see anything different. The TV was blaring. The usual bottles of pills and liquor bottles were there on the coffee table. Mom was passed out on the couch. Everything seemed normal until I saw pills scattered across the coffee table and some on the floor.

"Then, I looked at Mom's face. It was gray. Mom often didn't look well, but this was different. It was really gray!

"I don't remember much after that. I must have told Dad that Mom was dead and talked to the police when they arrived, but that part is all a blur.

"Even having the fire department show up didn't awaken me from a dazed stupor that lasted for weeks. I was like a zombie walking around.

"I didn't miss any school or football practice. I didn't tell anybody at school. I think it was maybe two weeks later, one of my teachers pulled me out of class and sent me to the school counselor. She had heard about my mom and was worried about me.

"The counselor asked a lot of questions and I guess it kind of woke me up. It was like waking up from a very bad dream, but still, I wasn't sad or depressed. I was just relieved.

"I felt guilty for feeling that way. I thought I should feel some grief or just be sad that my mom had died, but I guess I hadn't lost anything. My mom had been gone for years. She just finally quit breathing and I was glad. I was happy not to have to be her parent anymore and I was happy for Dad. I envisioned us shooting our bows, having fun, and hunting together again.

"That never happened. Dad blamed himself for Mom's death and he never really recovered from that. I was hoping that Dad would be as relieved as I was that Mom was gone and that we didn't have to take care of her 24/7, but Dad knew her before.

"He was still in love with the version of Mom that I never knew. He still saw her smiling, laughing, shooting her bow, full of confidence and life. I had only known the version full of insecurity, depression, substance abuse, and death.

"Dad's alcoholism really got out of control after mom died. He tried to hide the extent of his addiction from me. I knew it was bad, but it really hit me when I was a senior in high school.

"I was actually a starter on the football team by then, a wide receiver. One day, I forgot my cleats and had to run home to get them before practice. There was a delivery truck in the driveway and they were unloading a pallet of boxes of alcohol. The boxes had my dad's name on them. The guy joked that we must be throwing some kind of party, but I didn't laugh. I realized that this was all for him and that his drinking was worse than I thought.

"The guy said he'd see me next month and it dawned on me that Dad had planned the alcohol deliveries for when I was away at school or at football practice. He must have been drinking himself into a stupor every day, but somehow keeping the extent of his problem hidden from me.

"Dad died six years later, in the same room that Mom had died in. I'm glad I wasn't there. I was away at fire academy.

"The cleaning crew found him, blood all over. At first, the police thought it was a crime scene with so much blood, but turns out, he had esophageal varices."

Jake spoke up, "What's that?"

"It's when someone consumes so much alcohol for so long that the veins in their esophagus can burst. My dad basically drowned in his own blood. The blood drained into his lungs and he coughed up so much blood in that room that the police were looking for knife or gunshot wounds on his body.

"I never went back into that room, even after the blood was cleaned up. It held too many bad memories. I had moved out several years earlier and I sold the house right after burying Dad.

"What happened to the girl?" Jake wondered out loud.

"Oh, Tanya? I'm going to need a nap before I tell you about Tanya."

"That's fair." Jake felt sorry for his patient as he watched him doze. He hoped to hear some good news from his new friend's story; that he had found love to offset his bad luck.

Chapter 11

After a couple hours of sleep, Ethan continued. "After we met at that summer camp, Tanya and I kept in touch, but Dad was pretty opposed to me dating someone of her socioeconomic status.

"I didn't think Dad was probably the best person to get relationship advice from, but still, I didn't want to add any more stress to his life, especially after Mom died.

"Tanya and I wrote letters and snuck in an occasional phone call. We dated other people, but we stayed in touch over the years. I believed that Tanya was the only girl that really seemed to love me for who I was. She would ask me all kinds of questions about my life. At the time, she seemed really into me and genuinely seemed to care.

"When Dad died, we started dating in earnest and I fell in love hard. Tanya was pretty and blonde and funny; always the life of the party. She could light up any room and she added light to my very dark life.

"It didn't take long before she had moved in with me at my apartment in Philly. I was a new firefighter. I loved my job. I loved my girlfriend and I loved my life.

"Tanya made everything fun. We partied every night, which made work very difficult. I was young and in love, so I made it work.

" I guess we had been living together for about two years when I had an incident at work. We had just finished working a structure fire and I was rolling up hose. The next thing I knew, I was waking up in the hospital. They told me I had passed out and had fallen into the gutter and curb on the street.

"Fortunately, I had my bunker gear on because my head had hit the curb hard. Even with the helmet on, I had gotten a pretty bad concussion.

"When I woke up at the hospital, Tanya was there. She didn't have a job, so she was by my side night and day for the two days that I was there.

"She was so supportive when the doc gave me the news that I hadn't passed out from dehydration, but that actually, my liver was failing. They had run some tests and found my liver failure, not surprisingly, due to my history with alcohol.

"It seems that if kids start drinking heavily when they're young, they're very susceptible to early liver disease. I guess my dad didn't think about that possibility when he had encouraged me to join him for drinks starting when I was seven.

"The doctor got me on a donor list for a new liver, but I had to stop drinking any form of alcohol immediately. Tanya took care of me at home for six months. Withdrawal symptoms were hell, but I was feeling pretty good about my chances as I was slowly working to the top of the donor list.

"The way the donor list works is that, if you stay sober, and others either get their donated liver or they pass away, you move closer to the top of the list; closer to your new liver and a new lease on life.

"I felt bad about it, but I found myself hoping that other people would die sooner so that I could live. Both the deaths of donors and those above me on the list would speed up the process of me getting my new liver.

"With Tanya there to love me, I needed to get better so that we could get back to living out our dreams together. My two passions, Tanya and firefighting, both needed me to be healthy.

"Tanya started pressuring me to get married. I was hesitant at first because I didn't know the outcome of the surgery. I didn't want to leave her as a newlywed widow, but she insisted that she didn't care. She said that even if I died, she would rather have two months as the wife of the man she loved then regret never marrying me.

"I felt like the luckiest man alive, having someone who would love me through this sickness so selflessly. We started making wedding plans.

"One day, when Tanya was out getting some groceries. I got a call from my financial advisor and investment broker. He told me that my dad had made some poor investments with his money right before he died, probably because his heavy drinking had caused him to be confused at times.

"He told me that he was able to get out of those investments if I gave him the go-ahead, but there was going to be a significant loss to my inheritance. It took a few weeks to know how bad it was, but once the dust had cleared, I had lost over 90% of my inheritance.

"When Tanya got home, I told her the news. To my surprise, she became furious. I'd never seen her like that. I tried to assure her that even if I couldn't get back to work right away, the money that was still invested in good stock and what I got for my father's company would give us about two hundred thousand a year. That would be plenty to live on.

"Two weeks later, I woke up to a goodbye note from her and all her stuff was gone from the apartment. The note said that my sickness had just become too hard for her to deal with and she was calling off the engagement. Seems that she was more in love with my money than with me.

"Just a month later, I learned that she had already hooked up with another guy who was a doctor and drove a Porsche. Hopefully, that works out for her.

"I immediately turned to my friend, the bottle, for a three-day binge. Unfortunately, the alcohol was still in my bloodstream the next time I had blood work done during dialysis. I got kicked off the donor list. I tried to explain the circumstances, but I was too high a risk for wasting a good liver if I kept drinking, so I was dropped to the bottom of the list and had to start over.

"I was really depressed over losing Tanya and I had no friends. My family situation growing up hadn't allowed me the opportunity to know how to build normal friendships with people, so I still turned back to alcohol for comfort. I figured that I couldn't hurt a failing liver anyway.

"I would time it so that the alcohol would be out of my bloodstream before my next doctor's appointment and then I would drink again right after the appointment. That was working out okay until one day, I was so weak that I passed out in my apartment.

"I had hired a kid to bring me food every day and when I hadn't answered the door, he immediately called 911. I had been drinking recently and the ER discovered that I had a high level of alcohol in my blood when I was brought in. Because of that, I was dropped again to the bottom of the list. I decided that I shouldn't even be on the list, possibly keeping someone else from living the life they deserved. I asked them to just take me off the donor list.

"That's when I decided to come out here before I got too weak. I wanted to remember the good times that my family had here and then die on my own terms. Guess that part didn't work out so well."

Jake wondered at the seeming lack of self-pity in Ethan as he told his story. "Oh, man! I'm so sorry you had to go through all that."

"Nah, I'm good," Ethan replied. "Wasn't your fault, was it?" he said, smiling.

Ethan fell back to sleep while Jake finished his shift. He couldn't believe that someone like Tanya could seem so loving and caring, but then totally drop Ethan when he had lost his money. It seemed to

Jake that Ethan's wealth had nothing to do with how much money he had, but everything to do with his character. Here was someone who had become a firefighter to selflessly help others even though he didn't have to work to make a living. Tanya was a fool.

Chapter 12

The following night, Jake was running a bit late. Or rather, he wasn't his usual fifteen minutes early, so he just caught a glimpse of Molly as she was driving away from the hospital. In truth, he had timed his arrival so that he wouldn't interact with Molly tonight. He was hoping that she would warm up a bit to him if he gave her some space.

Ethan was awake and sitting up in his bed when Jake got to his room. Jake thought Ethan's skin color looked better.

"Hey, you look like you're feeling better."

Ethan smiled and nodded. "I'll take it when I can. I know there's some not-so-fun days coming. Without a transplant, my days are numbered."

"So, what's up with that?", Jake asked. "Is there a way that you could still get a new liver?"

Ethan paused a few seconds and thought about it before answering. "Well, I guess I haven't burnt my bridges here in Colorado. Technically, if there's a local donor that dies in the next few weeks or months, I guess it's possible. I'm not really holding out hope."

"Well, I'm going to ask your doctor how that works and see what the process is," Jake promised. "I'm going to get you on a donor list. A Colorado liver is probably healthier than an east coast liver anyway."

Ethan laughed and then responded wearily, "Knock yourself out. In the meantime, I feel like I've been pulling more than my share of the story duties. Tonight, I want to hear your story."

"Okay," Jake replied. "What do you want to know?"

"How about you tell me why you reacted when I mentioned 9/11."

Jake hadn't told very many people about what had happened in his life that day. Somehow, he felt he could trust Ethan with this most painful memory.

He began, "When I was a kid, I lived in New York. Well actually, Jersey, but we did everything in the city. Like you, I'm also an only child. My dad was a cop, a detective for NYPD. My mom stopped working when I was born because she wanted to spend time raising me, but she started working again when I was thirteen. I could take care of myself at that point.

"I remember how excited Mom was when she got her new job about a month before my birthday in 2001. She was a receptionist for some big company in the city. I didn't pay much attention to what her job was when she told me. I was just excited to have more freedom. I felt more grown up that mom trusted me to take public transport and get myself home when both my parents were working.

"In the fall, I was going into the eighth grade and I was excited about starting at a new school. Since mom was now also working, my parents could afford to send me to a private school that year.

"If I knew what would happen, I would have begged her not to work. I would have gone to the worst school in New York to keep her at home.

"That Tuesday morning, I remember being at school and getting a strange page from Dad. Remember pagers? I had one so that Mom and Dad could message me at school. This was back before every kid had a phone.

"The message said, 'Gotta check on Mom. Love you, Son!' The time was 9:10. I think I read that page thousands of times in the next several years before that pager died.

"When I got the page, I was in my second class of the day. A few minutes later, in class, our teacher told us about the attack on the World Trade Center. I ran out of the school. Several teachers tried to stop me, but I had to find out if Mom was safe. I got home and turned on the TV just in time to see the South Tower collapse live.

"I prayed that Mom didn't work anywhere close to there, but I actually had no idea where her office was. After trying to call her work phone, I frantically searched her desk until I found a pay stub that gave her work address as the World Trade Center, South Tower.

"I waited by the phone all day and all that night for a call from my mom or dad that never came. The next day, I called my dad's office phone which was answered by another NYPD detective.

"She told me that she and Dad had been working a case within a mile of the trade centers when they heard about the attack. He had taken off running toward the towers. The last radio traffic from him at 9:20 was that he had arrived on scene and was entering the South Tower. Forty minutes later, the building collapsed.

"I held out hope that somehow my parents had survived. I had called all the hospitals in the area, hoping that I hadn't heard from them because they were just unconscious, but okay, recovering in a hospital bed somewhere.

"In all the chaos surrounding the attack, nobody had thought to check on me. I guess nobody knew that both my parents had died that day. I wasn't the only student that just didn't show up for school after the chaos of the attacks in the city, so no one thought it was unusual.

"After two weeks, I had run out of food at home and I finally called my dad's work number again. I asked what I should do if I thought both of my parents had died in the attack. They sent social services out and I ended up in Boston with a fifty-year-old lady. She was a cousin of my mom's that I had never met.

"Kathy tried to take care of me, but she was never married or had kids. She had no idea what to do with an angry teenager who had just lost both of his parents.

"It was such a crazy way to lose someone. I had no proof that they were dead. I saw no bodies. There was no funeral; no grave. They were there on Monday and they were gone on Tuesday. No goodbyes. I don't even remember my last conversations with them.

"Kathy tried her best, but by summer it was obvious to her and social services that it wasn't working. I skipped school more days than I attended that year and I had even run away twice.

"The first time, I was caught, but the second time, I managed by bus to make it from Boston to New York. I got all the way to ground zero before someone noticed me sneaking around and called the cops.

"Ironically, the police officer who caught me had known my dad. He talked to me for hours about working with Dad and what a great cop he was. He actually got permission to come in off the street to talk to me at the station to make sure I was okay. He stayed with me until social services picked me up to take me back to Boston.

"After that, they contacted Uncle Peter out here in Colorado. He agreed to take me right away.

"I didn't know much about Uncle Peter. I guess he had come to see me when I was born, but I only remember him from when he came to my eighth birthday party.

"He seemed strange to me, dressed in a flannel shirt and a wool vest, sporting a big bushy beard. He was definitely out of place in the city, this mountain man from Colorado.

"But, he was the best caretaker I could have asked for. I gave him plenty of grief and he was strict with me, but I also knew that he loved me, almost from day one."

Jake told Ethan about the transition from city life to living in the mountains, not even in a town, but in a cabin outside of Grand Lake. He talked about starting school that first year and how he was held back because of his poor attendance in Boston.

"That turned out to be the best part of that time in my life, having to do eighth grade again."

"Why?" Ethan wondered aloud.

"Because Molly was in eighth grade in 2002. She became my friend, she changed my life, and she eventually became my girlfriend."

"Wait a minute," Ethan interjected. "You're not talking about that cute nurse, Molly, who works here, are you? The sweet brunette with the intense eyes?"

"Prettiest girl in the world!" Jake replied. Jake told about how they had met in middle school and how she had given him the journal for Christmas. He related how much that journal had helped him to process the loss of his parents and even just to understand who he was and what kind of person he wanted to be.

"I didn't talk to anyone about how I was feeling unless I first wrote out my thoughts in that journal. Even then, I only really talked to Molly, and sometimes, my Uncle Peter."

"Molly and I dated all through high school. She even started writing out our life plan. I remember, she bought a new green notebook and wrote 'J&M-The PLAN' with a sharpie on the front cover. She wrote out how we would graduate from high school and then what we would do for work.

"She wanted to become a nurse. She researched how to become a nurse, how long it would take, and where to go to school. She figured out how much school would cost. She saved nearly every penny from her summer job working for an ice cream shop in Grand Lake to pay for it. I think she worked that ice cream job for five years.

"I wanted to work outside. My uncle had worked for Rocky as a munitions expert after he got out of the army. He helped me get seasonal work on trail crew in the summers. He still knew a lot of employees at the Park at that time even though he had retired years earlier. That made it easier for me to get hired.

"Uncle Peter had lost use of his right hand from a blasting cap incident working with a new employee who didn't know what he was doing. Peter was what the Park calls a 'master blaster', but his injury caused him to retire early before I came to live with him.

"Molly wrote out a timeline in the notebook detailing when we would get to each of our career goals and then, at the end of the timeline, with no specific date, she wrote 'wedding.'

"Everything was going according to her plan until about two years ago. Molly had worked hard and become a nurse and I had worked my way up to being a law enforcement ranger with the Park.

"I loved my job. It was the perfect mix for my personality with some time alone on the trail and some interaction with people.

"I often helped with carry outs if someone was injured in the Park since I'm certified as a wilderness EMT. I loved that part of my job.

"Anyway, on June 20th, 2014, I was assisting with a patient who had been thrown from a horse about two miles back on the Timber Lake trail. Ironically, the patient had a broken leg. I wasn't paying attention to where my feet were and two other members of the litter team slipped on a steep section of the trail at the same time.

"I was able to catch the litter and the patient, but my foot got wedged between two rocks and I broke my leg; complete tib/fib open fracture. Not a good day for me or the other patient as they had to organize two new teams to get us both out. We got caught in an afternoon thunderstorm and were both pretty hypothermic before they got us out."

"How did your injury mess with Molly's plan?" Ethan wondered out loud.

Jake continued, "I already had a ring and was just waiting for the perfect time to propose. When I got hurt, I wanted to wait until I had healed up so that I could get down on one knee. I figured we would be engaged by the end of summer, but I knew that Molly wanted to be surprised, so I never told her about my plan to propose.

"My surgery was down in Denver. It went well, but they had me on a really high dose of pain meds for weeks as I recovered. I didn't even realize this could happen, but by the time my leg was healed, I was totally addicted to the meds.

"I started doing crazy stuff like forging doctor signatures to get more meds than what I was supposed to have. I lost sight of everything except that next dose of pain meds. Even after the pain had subsided, I had such an intense craving for the drugs that I couldn't break free from them."

Jake told Ethan about the incident at the football game that had totally changed his life. He told about how it had cost him both his job and Molly.

"She stuck by me through everything, even as I got worse, but the football game really scared her. I guess that was the last straw for her.

"I'm trying to win her back, but I don't see how she can forgive me or trust me after that. I also don't know if I can live without Molly."

"Wow! That's quite a story." Ethan said softly. He was contemplative. "I realized a couple of things as you were telling your story.

"Number one, we both have a lot of significant things that have happened to us in the Septembers of our lives. Since 9/11, I always come into September wondering what's going to happen? Will it be good or bad this year?

"Every time something happens to me in September, I think 'It figures…it's always September.' Everything big seems to happen to me in September.

"Also, listening to your story, I think I need to start journaling. Maybe I could sort out some of my stuff by writing it down. If I give you some money, do you think you could buy me a notebook and bring it back to me here?"

"Absolutely!" Jake promised. "I'll get you one as soon as I get off and I'll bring it back this morning so you can start today."

Jake glanced out the window and noticed that it was starting to get light outside. Ethan followed his gaze and suddenly realized how tired he was. They both had been so engrossed in the story that the night had flown by.

The hour of Jake's shift that remained was spent with Ethan sleeping and Jake reliving his life in his thoughts, especially his regrets. He hadn't ever told anyone his whole story from start to finish before and it had brought some clarity to him. It had also given him a sense of hopelessness, extreme grief, and regret that he had messed up Molly's plan; their plan.

On the drive home that morning, Jake decided that it was time to bite the bullet and talk to Molly about where they stood.

Maybe tonight, before work, he could catch her after her shift. He didn't sleep well that morning. Anxiety kept him awake in spite of being wiped out from the long night.

Chapter 13

Jake went on an extra long run the next day to blow off some steam and calm his nerves. Everything, for him, was riding on Molly's response.

At times, he felt a thread of hope that she might change her mind and accept him back into her life, but then despair would fill his whole being as he imagined her rejection and what that would do to him.

After his run and shower, he talked all this through to himself as he wrote in his journal. It gave him a fleeting moment of calm to be able to face Molly and her decision. He knew he should make sure that he was clear-headed when he spoke to her, but inside, he was desperate, and his thoughts were wild, chaotic, and irrational.

He felt like he was standing at the top of Adams Falls teetering on the knife edge of a rock with no capacity to keep himself from plunging into the icy waters that would sweep him away to his death. "That dream was too real," he thought to himself.

Even though he had promised himself that he would abstain from drugs and alcohol, he took a little "liquid courage" from his uncle's old stash of vodka that he kept out in the shed with his blasting supplies. Uncle Peter used to calm himself with a few swigs of vodka if he had an intimidating blasting job to do.

Jake hated the stuff, but needed something to help him calm down without his breath smelling of alcohol. Vodka was good for that. He choked down a few swallows and felt that his nerves were slightly sedated.

In the end, it didn't matter as Molly wasn't at the hospital when he arrived that evening. At the nurses station, when he checked in for work, Hannah informed him that Molly was at a manager's meeting off-site.

She also said that Ethan had finished his seventy-two hour mental health hold, that he had signed a refusal for further treatment, and that he had checked himself out AMA. Jake remembered from his EMT training that AMA stood for "Against Medical Advice."

"Well, did he say where he was going?" Jake asked impatiently.

Hannah answered him flippantly, "No, not really but... oh yeah, he said to give you this." She held out a sticky note that had a phone number on it.

Part of Jake's duties when he wasn't locked down on a mental health patient was to make rounds, so when he was outside walking the perimeter of the hospital property, he called the number.

Ethan answered, "Hi Jake!"

"Wait! How did you know it was me?" Jake wondered aloud.

"Nobody else has this number. It's the landline here at the house."

"Fair enough."

Ethan's voice sounded strong. "Hey, I'm feeling pretty good today and want to do something after being cooped up in that hospital the last 3 days.

"Do you have any gardening tools that I could borrow? My dad always paid landscapers to keep the yard up, but I would like to feel useful."

Jake was glad to hear the strength and hope in his new friend's voice and tried to borrow it for his own situation. "Yeah, there's a bunch of tools in the shed behind my cabin. Help yourself. I don't keep anything locked."

He had told Ethan that his family's house was on the same road where his uncle's cabin was, just a few doors down.

"Thanks man," Ethan responded. "I owe you one. See ya."

Jake hung up, briefly wondering about what Ethan was going to do now. It sounded like he might stick around a while instead of going back to PA if he was planning on doing yard work at his house.

Thoughts of Molly and their upcoming conversation quickly caused Jake to neglect thoughts of Ethan. Until the issue with Molly was resolved, her response, and what it meant for his future, monopolized all of his thoughts tonight.

Jake tried to stay focused on his work throughout the night. He resolved to catch Molly in the parking lot in the morning to ask where they stood. His nerves were shot as the sun peeked over the mountains.

Jake's shift ended long before Molly's started, so he sat on the hood of his Cruiser, waiting. He noticed his hands shaking as Molly's car slowly pulled into the parking lot. He could use a shot of that vodka now.

She spotted the Cruiser right away and braced for the inevitable. The sun shone off of her long brown hair as she walked over towards him and he fell in love all over again in spite of her unflattering nurse scrubs.

The wind whipped her hair around into her face as she got closer. Jake knew she hated that. She usually had her hair tied back when she was outside, but he loved the way it looked, dancing with the wind.

"M, I need to talk to you," he started.

"Jake, wait," Molly cut in. "Before you say anything, I...I have to tell you...um...I'm dating someone."

"What!?"

"Yeah, so, we've been dating for a month."

Jake was totally blindsided. Neither one of them had dated anyone else since the eighth grade.

"Jake, I want Mike and I to…"

"Mike!? Mike who?" Jake demanded emphatically.

Molly lowered her voice, trying to temper the emotion in Jake's voice. "Mike Anderson, Jake."

"Mike Anderson!" Jake was struggling to control his voice. They both noticed other hospital employees glancing their way as they walked across the parking lot.

"Mike is…", Jake began. He was going to say "not your type", but Molly interrupted.

"Mike is stable, Jake. I think I just need something stable right now. Please, Jake. I just need you to give us some space. Give Mike and I a chance to figure out if we're right for each other."

"WE are right, M!" Jake's voice quivering as tears started to form. "We were always right."

"I've got to go to work." Molly turned before Jake could see her own tears forming. "Goodbye, Jake," she said softly over her shoulder as she quickly spun away.

That's not at all how Jake had intended the conversation to go. Despair and devastation filled him to such an extent that he was barely able to collect himself to drive away. He found an empty parking lot a few blocks away and took out his frustrations yelling and pounding his steering wheel.

The same anger and hopelessness that had consumed him when his parents had died flooded over him again. Back then, Molly had been his lifeline. She had saved him. She taught him how to write out his thoughts in his journal. She had helped him find purpose again.

The same feelings of despair from 2001 filled his heart again. It seemed the curse of 9/11 had found him once again, but now, with no Uncle Peter and no Molly to help him find his way out of it.

With hardly a conscious thought, Jake pointed his Cruiser toward the liquor store. Twenty minutes later, with a big box full of bottles, he grabbed a wine bottle off the top and held it high in the air toward the cashier.

"To Mike and Molly," he toasted with a fake smile.

"Mike and Molly," repeated the confused cashier holding an imaginary wine glass high. She had incorrectly assumed that Jake was in charge of the wine for a wedding and added, "May they live happily ever after!"

Jake's smile quickly faded. He turned and hit the door open so hard it broke the closer, but he didn't stop to fix it. Tearing out of the gravel lot, his tires spit rocks at the building, fortunately striking the block wall and not the windows.

"Hey! What's your problem?" The cashier yelled, even though she knew the question would never reach her unknown, belligerent customer.

She was new to the area, but had already heard of "Jake's mistake." After he left, she remembered that someone had told her about Jake's red Cruiser and she put two and two together.

"He really is crazy!" she muttered to herself as she surveyed the broken door.

Chapter 14

Molly had to take some time to compose herself in the employee bathroom before starting her shift. She wondered if she was making a mistake by totally breaking things off with Jake, but they had been together for so long, she wanted to test the waters a little bit and see what it was like to date someone else.

That sounded wrong, even in her head when she said it to herself. Things were going well with Mike though, so she told herself that she was doing the right thing. She just hated seeing Jake hurting, knowing that she was the cause for his pain.

"Think about it after you go home," she whispered a command to her reflection in the mirror. Thankful that she didn't wear makeup, she splashed cold water on her face in an effort to disguise her emotional state, took a deep breath, and made her way to the nurse's station.

The night shift charge nurse was busy with a patient, so Molly asked Hannah how the night had gone.

"Pretty good, really," Hannah chirped, too perky for someone who had been up all night. "I got to see more of that hot security guard since he was doing rounds last night."

Molly felt her face flush red as another wave of regret flooded over her. Something she hadn't considered was Jacob maybe dating someone else. She audibly gasped just under her breath, but Hannah caught it.

"What?"

"Um, I uh…just remembered something I need to do next week," Molly lied.

She imagined seeing Hannah and Jacob together, going out to dinner and a movie. She almost got physically sick.

"Are you okay? You look super-pale, Molly."

Quickly composing herself, Molly retreated a few steps and turned on her heels. "No, I'm good. I'm just going to check on room three real quick."

"Um, no, he's…" Hannah was trailing Molly as she entered Ethan's room, all clean and ready for the next patient.

Molly spun around abruptly to face Hannah. "Where's the patient?" she demanded, her harshness now revealing her fragile emotional state.

"Oh, I…" Hannah took a step back, trying to make sense of Molly's behavior, normally so professional and calm. "He uh, he's gone. He checked himself out AMA. It's good though. I had him sign a patient refusal and his seventy-two hour hold is up."

"Always check in with me," Molly snapped, "before letting someone sign a refusal AMA!" She stormed out of the room and down the hall. "…especially a mental health patient," she added over her shoulder.

Molly knew that she had been too harsh with Hannah, who had been following protocol with the patient refusal. She didn't apologize for her overreaction, though. She was even a bit pleased to see the perplexed look on Hannah's face as she silently packed up her things to finish up her shift.

Jealousy was a new feeling for Molly. Jake had been hers and everyone in Grand County knew it. Other girls in high school and several female Park employees had tried to turn his head, but he seemed to only have eyes for her. This feeling was something new and she didn't like it.

Molly started feeling guilty about how she had talked to Hannah and also earlier with Jake, but she quickly got into her work and was able to push aside her personal life to be figured out later.

Several hours later, Molly was on her laptop working on a patient report, trying hard not to think about Jake. It was impossible to ignore her thoughts, but she had to get through her work day.

It wasn't unusual for the nursing staff of the small rural hospital to stop what they were doing and listen when they heard some radio traffic on the scanner. Molly wasn't paying attention as she was trying to concentrate on her report.

Her head snapped up as she heard another nurse exclaim, "What did they say?" Molly tuned in her ears to the radio in time to hear the traffic from Grand County dispatch.

"ROMO is requesting back-up for a possible explosion near the Kawuneeche Visitor Center."

The small group of hospital staff all stopped what they were doing and gathered around the nurses station radio to listen. Molly scrambled to the radio to start scanning ROMO, the call sign for the dispatch center at Rocky Mountain National Park.

She got the radio switched to the right frequency in time to hear, "...heard a loud explosion near the visitor center. Possibly coming from the parking area."

"Copy that. Responding emergent from Timber Creek Campground." A few seconds ticked by before, "Confirming Grand County has backup en route?"

"Affirm. They have a unit en route from Grand Lake, emergent. ETA seven minutes."

Two hospital custodians and the three nurses on duty barely breathed as they listened for the next radio traffic. It was unusual for the Park to ask for assistance. They were usually pretty reluctant to ask for outside help, so everyone knew that something unusual was going on in the Park.

The radio crackled again. "I've dispatched fire and ambulance to the scene."

"Copy that. I'm two minutes out. Have them stage until I can secure the scene."

Two minutes seemed like a long time for the hospital staff. They started to wonder if they should get back to work, but nobody moved.

As the charge nurse, Molly wondered if she should break everyone up and ask them to return to work, but she figured there wasn't anything more pressing, so she allowed the impromptu conference to continue in silence.

The radio crackled to life again as the park ranger keyed his mic. "Show me arrival at KVC. I've got command. Looks like we have a late model red four-by-four in the south end of the lot. It appears a tree is scorched above it, but no active fire at this time. I'll be out to investigate."

Chapter 15

Frank had been a law enforcement ranger at Rocky for seventeen years. He had seen his share of injuries from car accidents, horse wrecks, hiking, rock climbing accidents, and even suicides, but nothing could prepare him for what he saw in the parking lot that day.

As he carefully approached the vehicle, he recognized the distinctive red Toyota Cruiser of his former co-worker. To make sure, he circled slightly in from the rear to see the license plate. Noting "JKSJEEP", his heart sank.

He could see blood splattered on the inside of all the windows and a basketball-sized hole in the roof, the metal curling outwards. Coming around to the passenger side door, Frank looked in through a bloodied window to see a body slumped over on the driver side seat. He noticed a green pipe-like T-post driver placed upside down on the floor beneath the steering wheel with the open side facing up.

He also noticed the Park service uniform and Jake's name tag on it. He looked for his friend's face, but it was gone. The blast had nearly obliterated his head and Frank remembered what Jake's uncle used to do for the Park.

He quickly determined that dynamite had been packed into the big pipe of the post driver which had concentrated all of that force upward. Frank noticed the lingering smell of recently expended dynamite mixed with the smell of blood and brain matter, even from outside the vehicle. He felt sick.

"ROMO, you can cancel fire and ambulance. We have a confirmed code black here. Call the coroner, please."

Frank took a minute to throw up before he opened the door. He saw that Jake's Park service hat and wallet were sitting on the passenger seat. He opened the wallet, pulled out the driver's license, and then keyed his radio mic again, "ROMO, please have the ambulance continue in non-emergent."

Frank saw that Jake's driver's license indicated that he was an organ donor. Maybe, if they acted quickly, something good could come from this tragedy and Jake's organs could, at least, be harvested to save someone else's life.

He retrieved his camera from his car to document the gory scene while he waited for the county coroner and the ambulance who would take the body for organ harvesting. Even though his head was gone, the rest of his body was intact from the blast.

Usually with suicides that happened in the Park, the body is in the backcountry, hours or days into decay when found. This was Frank's first opportunity to help with an organ donation and he wanted to make it count, if possible.

Frank's own sister had benefited from an organ donation three years earlier when her kidneys shut down, so this was personal, not just for the recipient, but since he knew Jake, it was personal from the donor side as well.

"Man, if I don't have PTSD already..." Frank said to no one in particular. He thought about how long he had until retirement as he noticed the coroner's vehicle and the ambulance arriving simultaneously.

He had only taken the first picture of the license plate when the coroner walked up and wanted a report. Frank pulled himself together and forced himself to act professionally until he could find time to process the trauma and grief from the call.

Chapter 16

Several months later:

Journal entry: "September 11, 2016 Never Summer Wilderness. Wow. September 11th. Seems like a good day for a new beginning. Fifteen years since that fateful day that marked my life so profoundly. Maybe it's time to redeem this day.

Fifteen years ago, it was a devastating day. Maybe, I should start expecting it to bring good luck now..."

Ethan wrote in his journal with more optimism than he felt. He took a minute to remember his friend who had also suffered so much from the 9/11 attack and who had sacrificed so much to help him live on.

He did feel stronger now. His time alone in the woods mixed with sore muscles from cutting and packing meat yesterday made him very tired, but deeply content.

The idea that had popped into his head last night was intriguing. If he dried the elk meat and used it as his primary food source, would it be possible to just hike into the woods and disappear for a while?

He was sure he wouldn't be missed and maybe it would give him a chance to wrap his head around what he wanted to do next.

While cutting the meat into thin strips to dry in the sun, he wondered how many native Americans had done this same thing in these mountains with the elk they shot with their bows.

The simple and timeless act of preserving meat through drying gave him a sense of satisfaction and freedom that he hadn't felt since he was a small child. The smile on his face as he worked would have been contagious if someone else had been there to see it.

Ethan made a drying rack out of the abundant lodgepole pine to keep the meat out of reach of the smaller forest animals and allow air to circulate around the meat.

Birds were a constant nuisance, so he built several smudge fires around the meat with punky logs to dissuade them in their efforts of thievery. The birds didn't like the smoke, so they stayed clear, but he still lost a few morsels to the bravest of the avian thieves, the gray jay.

The third night, he was glad for the fires as a bear had tried to sneak in and help himself to some of the meat. Ethan didn't want to have to shoot the bear as he didn't think he could carry more than the elk meat. He also wasn't sure if bear meat would dry well because of its higher fat content.

In the end, after several hours of keeping the fires high and throwing sticks and rocks at the bear, it wandered off into the forest to look for an easier meal. After that, Ethan kept a near-constant vigil at the drying racks to protect his meat.

Ethan was blessed with consistent wind and sunshine that worked together to dry the elk meat, but it still took a full week before it was fully cured. He had also used some alderwood in his fires to help preserve the meat and add a sweet smoky flavor.

When the meat was ready, it had lost over two-thirds of its weight and would last for a long time. Ethan thought it might sustain him for a month or more if he didn't allow it to get wet.

On the 20th of September, Ethan broke camp and shouldered the heavy pack. It weighed probably seventy or eighty pounds, but it felt good to have what he needed on his back; everything he needed to survive in the Rocky Mountains for the next four or five weeks alone.

He wasn't in a hurry as he didn't even know for sure where he was going. Plotting slowly northward up the Kawuneeche Valley, he reflected how his slow steps were a metaphor for his life going forward. As long as he just took the next step, not worrying about where it was taking him, but just leaning forward and moving his legs to catch his weight with each step, he would be all right. He hiked slowly, but with renewed purpose. He was hiking toward his new life.

Chapter 17

Evening was fast approaching for Ethan as he arrived at the Bowen/Baker trailhead. He waited just off the trail in the willows to avoid detection. He still didn't want to meet anyone and possibly have to answer their tricky questions.

As he waited, he took in the majesty of this place. He watched an osprey swoop down from its perch in a dead ponderosa tree. It dove straight into a deep pool in the river, its talons holding fast to a writhing Colorado River cutthroat trout that would be its dinner.

Ethan marveled at the design of the predatory bird. Built to be the perfect flying fisherman, the osprey can hunt fish larger than itself with its low weight and large wing surface area. Its ability to turn the fish head first for better aerodynamics was brilliant and fascinating. Somehow, watching the fishing success of that osprey gave Ethan infinite optimism for his own future.

Movement in the tall meadow grasses drew his attention away from the departing bird. A pair of coyotes were just beginning their nightly hunt. They were just thirty yards from Ethan, but upwind, so he was able to watch them without detection.

One of them paused for a few seconds, jumped high in the air and a few feet forward, thrusting his nose into the grass. When his head emerged, a lifeless ground squirrel hung from his sharp teeth. The other coyote joined its mate and they shared the small rodent with a few quick bites. They disappeared back into the grass to hunt together for their next meal.

Ethan leaned back onto his pack and closed his eyes for a quick nap before his hike that night. He was awakened with just enough light to make out what had made the splashing noise that had brought him out of his sleep.

A cow Shiras moose and her young calf were just crossing the river about seventy-five yards from him. They were moving his way so he took that as a sign to head out. They paused and stared when he stood up and hoisted his heavy pack up and around to his back.

"Alright, see ya," he said out loud to the moose as they stood transfixed, watching him walk away. Wary, but not frightened, they simply waited until he was gone and then continued looking for a place to bed down for the night.

Ethan made good time hiking north along the highway to the Colorado River trailhead. Only once did he have to dive into the ditch as a car approached. He laughed at himself as he struggled to stand back up again with the heavy pack. He had ended up with his feet higher than his head and most of the pack's weight up on his neck, pushing his head down into the pine duff. "At least it wasn't rocky," he thought.

As he got up though, he noticed a sting to his right wrist. A sharp stick had punctured his skin. He looked at it briefly with his headlamp and was glad it wasn't bleeding a lot.

Once he turned onto the Colorado River trail he found some pine resin to use as an antiseptic. He smeared it on the wound and then covered it with a makeshift bandage by using a piece of clear medical tape that he had in his pack.

He kept hiking until he passed Lulu City, an abandoned mining town. Ethan wasn't superstitious about ghosts in a ghost town, but still, he wanted to camp a good distance away.

The next few days, he stayed there at his camp near Lulu City. He had some fishing line and hooks and was able to catch a few fish everyday, which were a welcome change to his diet. As much as he liked elk meat, already he wanted some variety to his meals and catching the fish allowed that.

His next camp was further north. He hiked all the way through the valley called Little Yellowstone to La Poudre Pass where water on the east side of the pass flows to the Atlantic and the west side to the Pacific.

From there, he headed cross-country to the northwest where he could set up a camp away from any roads or trails. There, he found several cooperative blue grouse that were a welcome addition to the larder after finding their demise at the end of a sharp and well-placed arrow.

Resting for a few days, he contemplated what his next move should be. He thought about heading back down the Colorado River Valley and returning to Grand County, but he had now crossed into the next county to the north and it just felt right to keep going.

Ethan climbed a nearby mountain to get his bearings as he was now off the maps that he had brought. He noticed a long mountain range pointing toward the northwest and decided to follow it to see where it took him.

A day and a half later, he found a highway and then a trailhead at the south end of that range. He sketched a map in his journal, copying the map on the trailhead sign.

He headed into what he now knew was the Rawah Wilderness which followed the Medicine Bow Range. "Perfect," he thought, knowing that no roads or motorized vehicles were allowed in the wilderness area and there would be fewer people to encounter.

Several days later, Ethan was deep in the wilderness area. He was startled awake early in the morning with a gunshot that echoed off the valley walls where he was camped. He quickly realized that it must be opening morning for one of Colorado's rifle hunting seasons.

His watch told him it was Saturday, but he had lost track of what day of the month it was. Now, he realized that it was October and the opening day of the first rifle season. He quickly broke camp and started north again.

He still wanted to avoid people as long as possible, but he would have to be careful sneaking around with rifle hunters looking for movement in the woods. He hoped everyone would be careful to identify their target before they pulled the trigger.

He remembered why he liked bow hunting so much. An archery hunter would only be shooting at something close, but rifles were another story.

Before the day was out, he had seen the bright orange vests of four different hunters, all of which he had been able to get around without detection. His desire to stay undetected made him nervous when he was seeing this many people in the woods.

Because of the hunters he was seeing, Ethan decided to find a secluded spot to wait out the season before moving on. He found a steep, heavily wooded canyon and set up his camp near the stream at the bottom. The nearest trail was more than a mile away and the dense forest would keep most people out of the canyon.

He remembered that the first Colorado rifle season was a short one. After Wednesday, he heard no more rifle shots. Thursday afternoon, he broke camp and turned again to the north.

A few weeks later, Ethan woke to four inches of snow on his tent. He didn't know exactly where he was, but he knew that he was on the east side of the Medicine Bow Range that he had been following and thought he must have traveled far enough north to be across the border into Wyoming.

It was now November, his meat was nearly gone, and Ethan knew it was time to return to civilization. He actually missed people and really craved foods like hamburgers and pancakes, but he wouldn't trade his time in the woods for anything.

He was a new man. The wilderness had not disappointed. Ethan felt none of the stress and anxiety from two months prior. He now felt a renewed sense of peace that his time in the backcountry had given him.

His beard had grown out and he knew that the few clothes he had must smell terrible. He decided to spend the day getting ready to leave the wilderness and then start the hike out tomorrow. He washed a set of clothes and hung them out on willow branches to dry. It was cold, but the sun had returned after the brief snow storm. The sunshine and the wind worked together to dry his clothes.

He planned to find the nearest trailhead, bathe in the nearest creek, change into his clean clothes, and then flag down a ride into the nearest town. That was the plan.

Chapter 18

Packing up camp the following morning, Ethan noticed how light his pack felt. He had lightened the load by eating through most of his food, but also, months on the trail had conditioned his muscles so that he barely felt the pack.

He found a canyon that went to the northeast and followed it along a river at the bottom. About two miles down the canyon, he noticed a trail on the other side of the river which would make the hike out much easier. The water was too swift and deep to wade, so he continued down the canyon until he found a tree across the water that he could cross.

Having done dozens of similar crossings in the last few months, Ethan was not concerned as he stepped out onto the log. He quickly realized his mistake. He should have tested the integrity of the log before committing to the crossing as he could hear it cracking under his weight.

Turning around on the log was tricky with a full pack, so Ethan hurried to get across. The log gave way as he hit the middle of the river, pitching him headfirst into the icy waters.

It took a minute to get his feet in front of him to protect himself from hitting the rocks as he was rushed downstream. The strength of the current rushed him downstream and pushed his head underwater several times as he fought to control his direction. His pack became waterlogged and held him under the water several times before the current finally deposited him into a shallow eddy about 200 yards downstream.

He caught a willow branch hanging over the water and pulled himself over to the rocky shore where the current couldn't pull him further downstream.

It seemed like forever, but it was probably about 5 minutes before Ethan caught his breath and started assessing his situation. His legs were still in the water, so he hoisted himself up onto a flat rock.

When he did, he felt a sharp pain in his right ankle. He gingerly worked his boot and sock off and saw that his whole foot and ankle were swollen in spite of still being cold from the dunking.

He could already start to see the discoloration as the bruising and swelling began. He must have injured it when he fell from the log, but he hadn't noticed it in all the confusion of trying to get out of the stream.

He wriggled out of his pack and found that everything was wet, but he was only missing a few arrows from his quiver strapped to the side of the pack. They must have been knocked loose and they now belonged to the river.

Ethan quickly put his foot back into the boot before it got too swollen to fit. He loosened up the laces a little bit, but wanted the boot to compress the ankles slightly to keep the swelling at bay. He wondered if it was broken or sprained. Either way, he was sure he couldn't walk on it anytime soon.

Fortunately, Ethan had gotten out of the river on the trail side, so he crawled toward the trail to try to find a place to build a fire. He was still hypothermic from the water and shaking badly.

It took nearly two hours to get a fire started. The first lighter that he tried had gotten wet and wouldn't hold a flame, so he tried his other one. It gave him a flame, but his fingers were too cold. He was shaking so badly that he couldn't keep it going long enough to light the tender bundle of tiny fir branches that he had gathered.

Finally, he found and added some dried sap to the tinder and was able to hold a lighter on it long enough to start a small flame. He had to be super careful as he added more branches to the fire because his hands were shaking so badly. Twice, he nearly extinguished the small flame as his jerky movements scattered the sticks, but he was able to keep it alive both times.

Eventually, Ethan was able to add larger and larger material to the fire. It started to dry his clothes a little and he wasn't shaking quite as badly. Exhausted, he laid down next to the fire and fell fast asleep. It had been 3 hours since getting out of the river and it was starting to get dark.

When Ethan awoke, he was shivering again. It was fully dark and his fire was nearly out. His watch told him that it was 10:30 and he thanked it for being water resistant as he stoked the fire back to life.

Even in his current serious situation, he laughed at himself. For the last several weeks, he had been talking to his gear as if it were people. "I need to get back to civilization before I'm completely crazy," he ironically remarked to his pocket knife as he used it to cut some paracord to string up a makeshift shelter.

He used the rainfly from his tent to make a lean-to because all of his gear was wet and the tent would need to dry out before it was usable again. He knew he needed to stay near the fire to keep it going throughout the night. His clothes were still wet and he was cold, but the fire had brought him out of the grip of hypothermia. Tending to the fire allowed him to get only a few hours of sleep that night.

The next day, it was windy and cold, but the sun was out, so Ethan hobbled around his camp, spreading his gear over every available tree limb to dry out. Assessing his ankle, he knew he would not be able to walk out until the pain level came down to a manageable level.

He tried tying a couple of branches to both sides of his ankle to splint it, but the pain was still unbearable when he put weight on it. The makeshift splint did keep the ankle stable though, which made the pain tolerable when he was still. His skin had turned the blue/green color of a fracture so he assumed that he had broken something. Every few hours, he scooted down to the river's edge to soak the ankle, using the same cold water that had broken it.

After three days, Ethan figured that he had better start down the trail no matter what. He was out of food and he knew that, without food for energy, he was going to just get weaker. If he didn't get out soon, he could get snowed in and his body wouldn't be found until spring.

He mentally prepared himself for the pain that he knew would come as he started out in the morning. He wasn't sure how fast he could move or even how far he had to go.

He went through his gear and made a pile of everything he could do without so that his pack could be as light as possible. He stashed the pile of gear in his tent that he had pitched at the base of a big fir tree. Using some orange flagging to mark the spot for later, he then tried to get some sleep under the makeshift lean-to. Tomorrow would be hell.

Chapter 19

Ethan woke up and started taking down his rain fly shelter as the sun cleared the ridge to the east. It only took him a few minutes to gather his things and pack to leave.

The rain fly, sleeping bag, compass, and a few other items went into the pack, but he was leaving most of his gear here. The main part of the tent, his cooking gear, his bow and arrows; anything that would slow him down and wasn't absolutely essential was left in the tent cache.

Balancing on his good leg, he shouldered the pack and grabbed his crutch, a forked branch he had fashioned into a crude, but workable crutch to assist his movement.

Gingerly, he tested out shuffling the crutch forward and then the awkward jump step with his left foot. The first few steps were excruciating as he could feel crepitus, the broken bone ends grinding together in his ankle.

After a few more steps, he willed himself to ignore the pain and simply concentrate on the next step. He looked ahead and found a small tree beside the trail, maybe twenty feet away. It took several minutes to get there, but he celebrated briefly before picking out his next milestone.

"Milestone…that's a funny word," he muttered to himself. "Why do we call reaching a goal, a milestone? I'll have to look that up sometime. For today, I guess I'll call it a yardstone since I can't even think about going a mile."

After nearly two hours, he looked back to see his progress. He could still see the flagging he had put up at his cache. Discouraged and tired already, he willed himself to keep picking his next goal, struggling to make it there, stopping for a brief celebratory break, and then picking his next goal. The uphill and downhill sections, the rocky steps, the loose gravel, and the uneven ground all were working to defeat the broken man.

Eight hours later, Ethan spotted a flat spot near the trail where he decided to stop for the night. He wasn't sure what lay ahead or if he could find another suitable spot to lie down.

There were no trees around, so he simply got into his sleeping bag, wrapped himself like a burrito into his rain fly, and fell into an exhausted and fitful sleep.

His leg throbbed with every heartbeat and occasionally a sharp pain made him wake and cry out. He knew that the exertion from the trail and movement on the unstable bones had probably caused a lot of swelling, but he didn't want to look at it; didn't want to see how bad it was. It didn't matter. He couldn't do anything about it. He just had to get up tomorrow and keep going.

The following day was much like the first, but he encountered an obstacle that took a lot of time to navigate. Mid-morning, he hobbled around a bend in the trail and saw it; a wide feeder stream that the trail went across.

It was both a blessing and a curse. He had run out of water the day before and had been getting leg cramps due to dehydration. One bout of cramps had nearly caused him to pass out from the pain it caused in his ankle.

When he got to the stream, he drank as much as he could before filling up his water bottle. Then came the arduous task of slowly and carefully picking his way through the turbulent water; his injured right foot and crutch first, and then a quick step with the left leg, hopefully to land in a stable position and not on a slippery rounded river rock. Twice, he fell and got totally drenched. Fortunately, both times he had been able to twist to land on his left side to protect his ankle.

Normally, to rock-hop a creek like this, Ethan knew, would be a quick thirty second task, if that. After an hour, he dragged himself, soaked and exhausted, up the other bank and collapsed to the side of the trail.

Without food for energy, he fell into a deep sleep. When he awoke an hour and a half later, he was shaking violently from being wet and hypothermic, but the nap had renewed his energy somewhat.

Ethan pushed on down the trail through the rest of the day. His progress was steady, but painstakingly slow for someone who could normally cover fifteen to twenty miles a day without overly exerting himself. By nightfall, his clothes were dry and he was able to sleep fitfully.

The third day back on the trail after his accident was more of a mental challenge for Ethan. His mind was telling him that he wasn't going to make it; that he was getting weaker and it was too far to make it out.

At one point in the day, the demon of pessimism nearly won. He collapsed on the ground and thought about giving up. He hadn't seen any signs of people on this trail and, at night, he couldn't make out any lights that would indicate he was any closer to help. For all he knew, he may be going the wrong way on this trail, further into the wilderness.

Ethan wondered how long it would take to starve if he just laid down here and went to sleep. He took out his *Leatherman,* felt the keen knife blade and contemplated how much quicker it would be to sever an artery, maybe the brachial artery on the inside of his arm or, better yet, the femoral on his injured leg.

The pain was already shooting up his leg. Maybe he wouldn't even feel a sharp, quick slice to the big blood vessel and he would bleed out quickly. Then, the pain would be gone, and so would he.

Emphatically, he shook his head and yelled out loud, "No!" He shoved the multi-tool back into his pack. Through clenched teeth, he told himself that if he was going to die, it wouldn't be by his own hand. If Mother Nature was going to kill him, she would have to do the deed herself.

He willed himself to get back up and keep hobbling down the trail, even after the sun went down. He didn't want to stop again because he didn't trust himself not to fall into despair. If he kept moving, he was focused on the pain and not on the impossibility of his situation.

As dusk descended into the woods, he came onto a trail junction. The trail he had been following ended in a T at a more defined trail. He was unsure in the dark which direction to take on the new trail, so he found a place close to the junction to bed down and wait for daybreak.

Hopefully, he could find some clue in the light of the morning to confirm which direction to take. Before drifting off to sleep, Ethan wondered if he would have the strength for another day on the trail or even enough strength to wake up in the morning.

Chapter 20

Ethan thought he was dreaming when he woke just before
daybreak. He thought that he had heard the rhythmic clack of horses
hooves as the metal horse shoes impacted the rocks on the trail.

His camp was about forty feet from the trail and slightly uphill. He
sat up quickly, still in his sleeping bag, and looked down the trail in
the direction of the sound. He made out the outline of horses, riders,
and headlamps about a hundred yards down the trail in the dim
pre-dawn light.

He had raised up too quickly and his exhaustion and dehydration
nearly caused him to lose consciousness. The sight of the horses and
riders faded away as his vision closed in and he blacked out. He
could feel himself getting close to fully passing out. Lying down
quickly and putting his knees up allowed him to stay conscious, but
his vision didn't return.

Ethan knew that his blood sugar and hydration were dangerously
low and they were conspiring together to knock him out. He also
knew that these riders might be his only hope for survival. He was
aware that they couldn't see his camp from the trail, especially in the
dark. His sleeping bag was surrounded by low bushes that blocked
the rider's view. He had to remain conscious to alert them to where
he was.

Waiting until the horses hooves were louder, he tried to yell,
"Help!" but was unable to. His mouth and throat were too dry to
make a sound and the only noise he could manage was more like a

mouse squeak than a human voice. It certainly wasn't loud enough to be heard above the sound of the horses, their hoof beats mingling with the squeak of saddle leather.

He wondered if the sound of those horses was going to be the last sound he would hear on earth as another wave of dizziness from the effort of trying to speak nearly caused him to pass out again.

Ethan breathed hard and willed himself to stay awake. He gathered all his strength and reached up to a dead sagebrush branch that was hanging above his head. He grabbed the branch and twisted it down with all his strength until it broke.

Fortunately, the branch was dry and made a loud crack just as the last horse, a loaded pack animal, was passing his camp. The horse heard the snap and, thinking it was a predator, side-stepped off the trail and pulled hard on the lead rope.

The rider, on his own horse in front of the pack horse, had his cowboy hat pulled down and was nearly asleep in the saddle. His only thought was getting down the trail and the hot breakfast that was waiting for him ahead.

He had not heard the stick break, but the lead rope, tied to his saddlehorn tightened and pulled sideways against his body, nearly knocking him from his horse. "Whoa, Buck. What's the matter with you?" He looked back at Buck, who was motionless and wide-eyed, staring uphill from the trail.

The cowboy's hand instinctively went to the Marlin lever-action .30-30 in his scabbard as he envisioned a mountain lion in mid-air, leaping at the horses. Instead, his headlamp beam flashed over what looked like a human hand and forearm, still grasping the stick, just before it fell limp behind the brush.

Ethan didn't wake again until being jostled awake bouncing down the trail. He found himself in a travois, two lodgepole pine rails with a canvas tarp tied between them. The poles were lashed to the same pack horse who's alertness had saved his life.

Through his squinted eyes, he could just make out a horse and rider who were following behind the makeshift litter, the rider making sure he wouldn't get bounced out of the travois onto the trail.

Ethan took a deep breath, aware now that he would make it. Grateful to these unknown heroes, he wanted to thank them, but in his weak state, he couldn't stay awake. He closed his eyes again, content to trust others to get him out of the mountains safely. "It's funny," he thought, just before losing consciousness again. "These mountains saved me, but now, I'm being saved from them."

Chapter 21

It was a full two days later when Ethan woke up. He could tell he was in a hospital room, but he couldn't tell where. All he could see out his window was blowing snow.

He sat up in bed, thinking he would go over to the window to get a better look, but he was too weak and lightheaded. He slumped back onto his pillow. How luxurious was a pillow after months of camping out?

His movements had caused an electrode to come loose and the cardiac monitor started beeping. A few seconds later, a nurse burst into the room, concern evident on her face.

"It's a good face. I like it." The line from Ethan's favorite Christmas movie, *It's a Wonderful Life,* popped into his head as if he had watched it yesterday, though it had been years.

The cute nurse was short, probably 5' 2" Ethan guessed, her eyes and hair sharing the same dark brown color. She looked hispanic and her name tag "Blanca" confirmed it.

She was asking him a barrage of questions, but Ethan had not talked to anyone in a while. He didn't yet trust his groggy brain to direct his unpracticed tongue to make coherent sounds. He managed a weak smile and a shrug and Blanca responded with her own smile and said, "No problem. Just rest," as she took his pulse.

Ethan glanced down at the dainty hand at his wrist and noticed that it was half the size of his. He also noticed the diamond on her ring ...ught about the lucky guy who had put it there. He silently congratulated him on finding a good one and smiled again at Blanca.

Blanca left the room and came back a few minutes later with Dr. Stewart. By then, Ethan's brain had cleared up a bit and his voice was working. Dr. Stewart told him that he had been found and rescued by the guides of Feathered Shaft Outfitters who were on their last pack out trip for the season.

They were packing out their elk camp. The tents, stoves, cots, axes, and all the gear that was needed in camp that they used to guide their clients on an elk hunt in the backcountry were on their pack horses when they had found Ethan.

He didn't remember talking to them out on the trail, but apparently he had been able to give them directions to where he had stashed his gear. One of the guides had ridden back, retrieved it, and his gear was in a pile in the corner of the hospital room.

The group had quickly rigged up a travois and hauled Ethan to the trailhead near Centennial, Wyoming. Now, he was at *Ivinson Memorial Hospital* in Laramie.

Dr. Stewart told Ethan that he wanted to monitor him for a few weeks. "We need to see how you do with normal foods instead of just an IV and also see how that ankle does."

He said that when Ethan had arrived, he was in pretty bad shape due to dehydration and malnutrition and if the hunting guides hadn't found him, he likely would have died within a few days. "Also, while you were unconscious, our orthopedic surgeon operated on your ankle, which was badly broken."

Dr. Stewart continued, "It seems to be doing well now. We have you on pain meds and it will take some physical therapy, but you should be able to start using it with a walking cast in a week or so."

Dr. Stewart continued talking to Ethan about his medical condition for about ten more minutes ending with, "Do you have any questions for me?"

Ethan had a lot of questions, but two were foremost on his mind. "Umm... How much is all this going to cost?"

Dr. Stewart cleared his throat. "Well, I don't typically have much information about that. That would be a question for our finance department but you..." He paused, looking down at Ethan's chart. "...You have very good insurance. It's all covered."

"Ok, cool, umm...my next question then is, can we drop the pain meds?"

Dr. Stewart looked surprised. "I guess, if you can tolerate the pain in your ankle, we can ease you off of it over the next few days."

"I would appreciate that. I think I would rather feel the pain than the effects of the meds."

"Okay, sure." Dr. Stewart gave Blanca some quick instructions for reducing doses and then turned back to Ethan. "Anything else?"

Ethan shook his head and the doctor finished the conversation by writing a note in the chart, walking out of the room, and saying, "I'll check in on you tomorrow, then." Blanca followed close behind.

Ethan shook his head in amazement, wondering how the doctor could do all those things at once. He was probably thinking about his next patient at the same time that he was talking to Ethan.

Multi-tasking was not one of Ethan's strengths. He knew that about himself. Instead, his ability to focus on a singular task with tenacity helped him with many things in his life. "Probably helped me survive out there," he thought just before he closed his eyes.

Suddenly, he was extremely tired. The short conversation with his nurse and doctor was more human interaction than he had had in several months and it wore him out. Ethan quickly dropped into another deep sleep that his body desperately needed.

When Ethan woke up again, it was dark, both outside and in his room. The dim monitor lights allowed him to look around and he noticed a food tray next to the bed. He suddenly realized how hungry he was, but was disappointed to find just crackers and some bone broth.

His stomach told him it wanted pizza and a hamburger, but his brain knew that he needed to take it slow with his eating. It surprised him how satisfying the broth and crackers were and as he slept again, it made him dream of eating an elk steak and fish in a beautiful mountain meadow.

Chapter 22

Within a week, Ethan had improved enough to start walking around the hospital. By day ten, he was driving everyone crazy asking when he could get out.

He asked for a razor and shaved off his months-long beard, but decided to keep the mustache. It made him look very different, but he decided to try it, at least for a while.

On day fourteen, Blanca brought a visitor into Ethan's room. "Good morning, Ethan. There's someone here to see you."

The man was a bit older than Ethan, maybe forty-five years old. His weathered face said that most of those years had been spent outdoors. He removed his black Stetson cowboy hat as he stepped into the room, obviously out of his element and nervous in the sterile hospital environment.

The man cleared his throat and began, "Hi, Ethan. I'm Cody Wilkins. I own Feathered Shaft Outfitters. The last time I saw you, you were in pretty bad shape. My guys told me where they found you when I met them at the trailhead."

As the two men shook hands, Ethan was reminded of the last time he had met someone in a hospital room who had turned out to be a great friend. Cody's firm handshake and forthright manner of speaking caused him to instantly like the man. Somehow, without knowing why, Ethan felt like he could trust Cody and that he was going to be a significant part of his life going forward.

Cody asked Ethan where he had come from and how long he was in the mountains alone. Ethan explained that he was kind of at a new season of his life and, after he had shot his elk in Colorado, he felt like he needed more time to clear his head and find some peace.

"Did you find it? I mean, did you find peace up there?" Cody pointed with his thumb out the window toward the mountains.

"Yeah, I think I did." They talked for thirty more minutes about the mountains, bow hunting, fly fishing, and backpacking before Cody cleared his throat again.

"Well, I find myself in need of another guide or two for next year. A few of my guys found other work in town that allows them to be with their family more. I saw your traditional bow, and I know how challenging it is to hunt with one, so I can guess that you enjoy the hunt even more than the kill. I stress that with my guides and clients that our trips are more about the adventure than about taking a big animal.

I also know that anybody who can survive out in the mountains by himself for a couple of months must know what he's doing. I need guides that are comfortable in the woods, can provide a quality adventure for my clients, and can bring them back out alive. Would you want to work for me, you know, once you're all healed up?"

Ethan didn't need time to think about it. He accepted the job on the spot and figured he could work out the details later.

So, with another firm handshake before Cody left his room, Ethan stepped into the next chapter of his life. There were many unknowns about the future, but he was optimistic that his life was about to get better.

Twenty days after being brought in on the verge of death, Ethan's doctor saw enough improvement in him that he released him from the hospital. He still limped a little as he made his way out to Cody's truck, but it was great to feel the cold fresh air on his face.

"Any chance you know a place we can get a strong cup of coffee and a big breakfast this morning?" Ethan asked as he slid into the passenger side door.

Cody laughed. "Yeah…I know a place. Let's get you a real Wyoming meal."

Chapter 23

Ethan's recovery was slower than he would have liked, but through that winter, his ankle healed and he was able to start getting into shape so that he could return to the mountains as a guide.

He was living near Centennial where Feathered Shaft Outfitters had a lodge and bunkhouse. The buildings were on fifty acres of land that they called "The Ranch," even though they kept the horses at another property.

The guides lived in the bunkhouse when they weren't out guiding. Cody allowed Ethan to stay there rent free while he was recovering, even though he hadn't yet worked for FSO.

By May, Ethan felt nearly as strong and fit as his old self. He threw himself into his work, determined to pay Cody back for his kindness by doing all he could to help FSO prosper.

Most of the clients for FSO came from big cities and did not have many outdoor skills. Ethan found that he really enjoyed teaching them about the outdoors. His people skills quickly made him one of the favorite guides at FSO. Cody consistently heard good reports from satisfied clients about how knowledgeable and good-natured Ethan was with the guests.

Spring and summer were filled with backcountry fishing trips, usually three to five days at a time. FSO had several seasonal camps set up with wall tents, cots, wood stoves; all the amenities for a comfortable, yet rustic adventure.

The backcountry camps were typically a ten to fifteen mile horseback ride into a pristine mountain lake. They were mostly in western Wyoming, but they also operated some camps up into Montana.

As much as Ethan enjoyed the fishing trips, he really thrived taking clients out hunting. True to its name, Feathered Shaft catered almost exclusively to archery hunters in the fall.

Being a bowhunter himself, Ethan knew the limitations of the bow. He worked hard to get his clients close to game and his optimistic attitude and excitement for the hunt was contagious. A missed opportunity on a big bull elk would turn into a great campfire story in the evening for the client and Ethan, ending with, "next time it will work. We'll get him tomorrow," and often they would.

The exception to FSOs archery-only hunts was ten days in September during the middle of the elk rut that Cody would set aside every year for wounded members of the military community. They would hunt with muzzleloading rifles if their disability made it impossible to shoot a bow. During the winter, Cody would do fundraising to create sponsorships for the veterans so that they wouldn't have to pay for their hunt.

The first time Ethan guided for the veteran hunt, he took out two veterans who had both been wounded in Iraq. Billy was from Michigan and Matt was from Georgia.

Billy had lost half of his right leg and his right eye when an IED had exploded during his second tour. He still got around fairly well and Ethan was impressed with his tenacity and good attitude.

"I was the lucky one," Billy confided back at camp after hunting with Ethan for several days. "Three of my buddies died that day. It was my fault. I was supposed to clear the road with a metal detector before we went through, but I was sleep deprived and got in a hurry. I missed one IED. The army lost three of its finest, and I lost a leg and an eye."

Matt was from Atlanta and told a similar story. His unit had been caught in a firefight and was pinned down in the open with little cover. A sniper had killed several soldiers with shots to the head and had hit Matt's upper arm, shattering the humerus. They were held there for three days before reinforcements arrived and they were rescued.

"On the second day, we finally located the sniper's position and our own sniper, William, got his shot. We called him Weasel Will because he was small and cunning.

"He had to wait until it was almost dark, inch his way fifty yards down a shallow ditch, and hit the only thing he could see, just the top of the sniper's head.

"Best shot I ever saw. I ranged it at six hundred and twenty yards. Weasel had to thread the needle between two bricks on a rooftop and hit within an inch at that distance. Heck of a shot!

"We were still pinned down by gunfire though, even after we took out the sniper. By the time help came, my arm was badly infected and had to be amputated at the shoulder.

"Weasel made it out unscathed, but was killed a month later when the rest of the unit got ambushed. The whole unit was wiped out. Everyone was killed. If I wouldn't have been injured, I would be dead. Who would have thought that a bullet to my arm would end up saving my life?"

Billy had come back to his high school sweetheart in Michigan, but she soon left him when his disabilities and mental health issues were too much for her to handle. Soon after they broke up, she had eloped with a mutual friend from high school. Billy suspected that they had started dating while he was away fighting for his country.

Matt told them that since middle school he had dreamed of becoming a surgeon. He had been a medic in the army and planned to pay for college and medical school through his military service.

97

Instead, he ended up with only one good hand and a nervous twitch that would make using a scalpel with any kind of skill impossible.

While waiting for elk in a blind at a water pond, all three men shared their lowest points in life; different things that had brought them close to taking their own life. They also shared where they now found hope and a reason to live.

Ethan now lived for guiding and found his peace in nature. Matt found a family at his church of people who loved him out of his depression. A young adults pastor there had become his best friend and was always there for him when he was dealing with depression and survivor's guilt.

Billy had a new girlfriend that loved him for who he was and not the fantasy of love that his high school sweetheart could no longer fit him into.

"I'm going to ask her when I get back," he said as he pulled a ring box out of his pocket to show them. "Brought this on the hunt for good luck."

It must have worked as Billy made a nice shot on a 5x5 bull elk on the fourth morning of the hunt. Matt would have also been able to take an elk with a muzzleloader, but he wanted to hunt with his crossbow and the elk never made it close enough for a clean shot.

He wasn't too disappointed. He had hunted the way he wanted to and Cody offered him another hunt with FSO the next year. Billy shared some of his meat with Matt and the two new friends vowed to stay in touch. Before the elk hunt had ended, they were already planning a hog hunt in Georgia together after the new year.

Chapter 24

After FSO had finished all of their hunts for the season, most of the guys went back to other jobs until the fishing trips started back up in the spring. Most of them worked in construction, but Cody asked Ethan if he would work for FSO through the winter.

Cody wanted to expand the business and needed Ethan to man some booths at sportsman shows that he couldn't personally make it to, essentially doubling their advertising potential for prospective clients. There was also work to be done in the off season getting gear ready and scouting for new areas to fish and hunt.

In December, Ethan was flying back from one of the shows in Dallas. It had been a good trip. He had talked to hundreds of people who were shopping for a guided fishing trip or a hunt.

A dozen had booked hunts for the next season and 15 had booked a wilderness fishing trip with FSO. Ethan had a list of many more interested clients that needed to be followed up on.

He was glad that FSO had an admin to do follow up with the clients so that he didn't have to. In fact, Cody's sister, Sheridan was the office administrator while her husband, James, was the head guide for the fishing trips.

Ethan liked the family atmosphere of the company since he didn't have a family of his own. He felt like he was starting to fit in with the FSO family and he really liked it. It felt like his own identity was more secure being part of a strong family unit.

Now, as he flew back from the show, he reclined his seat, pulled the rim of his cowboy hat down low, and closed his eyes. He had kept the mustache, and now, along with his hat and boots, he really looked the part of a Wyoming cowboy. He had some time to reflect as the steady hum of the jet engine somehow put him in a contemplative mood.

Ethan's first impressions of Cody had been correct. They had become very close friends even though Cody was his boss. Cody was the most generous person Ethan had ever known.

In July, Cody had treated his whole crew to two days at the Cheyenne Frontier Days, paying for hotel rooms, food, and all the festivities. He had taken everyone into a hat shop and bought them each a new custom Stetson cowboy hat.

Ethan touched the rim of his hat again and smiled. He had never worn a cowboy hat before, but it just felt right now that he lived in the cowboy state.

"What's her name?" a soft, sweet voice startled Ethan as his eyes snapped open.

"What the...?" Ethan tried to regain his composure.

The flight attendant had leaned over next to Ethan's ear so that she wouldn't disturb the other passengers, most of whom were asleep.

"Excuse me?" Ethan stammered.

"Hi. I'm Cassie," the young, blond attendant stated as she pointed to her name tag.

"Hi...I'm Ethan. Um...sorry...no name tag," he responded, pointing to his name-tagless chest. Cassie smiled and laughed softly.

Ethan continued, "What did you ask me?"

"Oh, usually when a cute guy is smiling in his sleep, he's thinking about a special girl. I asked what her name is."

"Ahh...nope, no girl. Sorry to disappoint you."

Cassie leaned close to his ear again and whispered, "I'm not disappointed." As she turned to walk toward the cockpit, she smiled and winked at Ethan.

About ten rows forward, she turned back and was clearly pleased to see him leaning slightly out into the aisle to follow her with his eyes. He caught another wink just before she turned back around to continue her work.

"Sassy little thing," Ethan thought to himself as he leaned back in his seat again. He pulled his hat even further down in the front, smiled, closed his eyes, and dozed off.

"We are beginning our final approach into DIA. All passengers, please return to your seats and fasten your seat belts as we begin our descent. Flight crew, please return to your seats and prepare for landing."

Ethan hadn't meant to sleep through the flight. He was only trying to rest his eyes for a bit, but figured he must have needed the rest. He noticed that his trash had been removed from his tray except for a folded napkin.

Opening it, he found a note: "I'm in Denver for a few days if you want to go get a drink or something. Cassie." A phone number was at the bottom of the napkin as was a "PS, I like your hat, cowboy."

After landing, Cassie was in the front of the plane with another flight attendant as the passengers disembarked. Ethan heard her cheerful voice even before he could see her through the crowd of passengers.

"Thank you for flying with us tonight. We hope to see you again soon." As he got closer, he noticed her kneel down to talk to a little boy who she had obviously had a conversation with during the flight.

"Hey, Tommy. It was nice to meet you. You're going to make a great pilot someday. Maybe I can be on your flight crew." The boy, maybe six or seven years old, beamed and started talking excitedly to his mom as they stepped off the plane.

"Mom! She remembered what I want to be when I grow up! She's nice! Hey, Mom! I think…" Ethan didn't catch the rest of what Tommy said as the mother and son turned into the boarding bridge. He agreed with the boy and thought to himself, "Yes, she is nice."

When he got up to where Cassie was, she said, "I hope you found everything to your liking today, sir." There was a slight emphasis on the word "found."

Ethan caught the hint and pulled the corner of the napkin just slightly out of his vest pocket. He smiled. "Yes, ma'am. I sure did. Thank you so much." He touched the front rim of his hat as Cassie's face flushed. She struggled to pull herself together to greet the next passengers.

He would text her tomorrow, apologize, say he had to get back to work right away, and end with, "Maybe next time." The back to work thing was true, but he knew that he wasn't going to pursue a "next time."

Cassie seemed great, but Ethan knew he wasn't ready for a relationship yet and didn't want to give her false hope. He had gone on a few dates in the last year, but it was only because Cody's wife, Jillian, was trying to set him up.

She meant well, so Ethan had gone out with the girls she had picked out for him, but his past had left his heart too raw to open it to a girl again, at least not yet. After the third failed attempt, Jillian had backed off.

Ethan hoped that he could, one day, settle down and get married, but he knew that he just wasn't ready yet. There was a part of him that was too broken. He had been too hurt. He didn't want to take that into another relationship until he did the work to get better emotionally. Right now, he didn't have time for that.

Chapter 25

Cody met Ethan in the arrivals area outside of baggage claim. Ethan was glad to jump in the warm truck as Denver welcomed him back with a strong, bitter wind from the northwest.

Dallas was a nice warm place to visit, but he was glad to get back to a less populated area. He loved people, but also needed time alone to recharge. Wyoming seemed to fit that bill for Ethan perfectly.

Cody had just finished working a show in Denver, so the two friends talked business for the first part of the two and a half hours home. They stopped for gas in Fort Collins at about 2:00 A.M. before continuing on up to Laramie.

Getting back on the road and pointing the truck north, Cody cleared his throat. Ethan had learned that when Cody cleared his throat it was his way of starting a conversation that maybe he was nervous about or he didn't know what the reaction would be.

"So, it's a few weeks before Christmas. Do you have any plans?"

Ethan hadn't celebrated Christmas for years, but didn't really want to get into that history with Cody, so he simply replied, "No, nothing planned yet."

"Well, Jillian wanted me to ask you if you wanted to join us for Christmas this year."

Cody and Jillian had three teenagers that all adored Ethan and treated him like an older brother. Spending time with their family was incredibly fun for Ethan, but it was also sometimes difficult. It would remind him that he didn't have the same kind of stable family growing up. He wondered about all he had missed as a kid, and maybe even what he was still missing now.

As uncomfortable as it could be, he still loved spending time with Cody's family. "I'd love to. Thank you, Cody."

When they got to Cody's house in Laramie in the wee hours of the morning, Ethan was glad that he had gotten some rest on the plane. He would need it as he drove the rest of the way to the bunkhouse. Cody grabbed Ethan's luggage from his truck bed and switched it over to Ethan's truck.

Actually, the truck belonged to FSO, but Ethan was free to use it for business or personal use. A nice F-250, it was made for hauling lots of gear or pulling horse trailers, but tonight, Ethan was looking forward to the heated leather seat.

"Take next week off, Ethan. You earned it. I'll text you about the Christmas plans."

"Sounds good, Cody. Thank you so much…for everything." They both understood that "everything" really meant everything to Ethan; his job, their friendship, even his life.

Pretty much everything he had, he owed to Cody and FSO, but Cody blew it off. "Ahh…it's nothing. Don't mention it. Go get some rest," he said and he tapped twice on the roof of the truck.

A few miles down the road, Ethan had to wipe a tear from his cheek. If anyone else was in the truck, he would have said something about his eyes watering from the cold. Since nobody else was there, he didn't say a word and he allowed a few ensuing tears of gratitude to run and fall without hindrance.

He normally didn't allow himself to get this emotional with people, but, for some reason, he was feeling especially raw and he was grateful to Cody for his generosity and friendship.

Chapter 26

A few weeks later, Ethan was at Cody's house for a Christmas Eve dinner. The family had a tradition of eating pizza just before going to their church for a Christmas Eve service. Ethan wasn't sure how the pizza tradition started, but the whole family was really into it, even Cody and Jillian.

Everyone got to pick out all the toppings for their own personal pizza and then bake and eat it. It was loud and raucous as jokes and toppings were flying. Everyone gave Cody a hard time for putting sardines on his pizza and he took the ribbing with a good-natured laugh. A small food fight broke out before Jillian stepped in and, half-seriously, threatened to cancel Christmas.

While the pizzas were baking, Cody gathered everyone in the living room and they all quieted down while Cody read the Christmas story from the Bible. Ethan was amazed that the teenagers were actually listening and being respectful, even though, he guessed, they probably heard this story every year.

Late that night, after getting back from the Christmas church service, Ethan lay awake on the bed in the spare room. He reflected on this family. Everyone seemed to know how valuable and loved they were.

They seemed confident in their identity and were able to express themselves according to their own individual personalities. Like the pizzas, everyone was unique and they were comfortable enough to create their own way, but all in the context and safety of the family.

Ethan realized that he had never been exposed to such stability and freedom before. He knew that Cody and Jillian were very strict with their kids, but somehow, maybe even because of those boundaries, each person in the family was thriving. Mentally and emotionally, this seemed like the perfect scenario for kids to grow up to be healthy.

He was going to experience even more of this family's traditions and practical displays of love tomorrow, but that night, as Ethan lay awake with his thoughts, a deep determination to someday create this with someone else started to take root in him. What he had not experienced growing up, he wanted to create for his future family.

Ethan talked to himself while he lay awake. "If I ever get serious about a girl, I need to pick Cody's brain about how all this works. What are the secrets? Maybe there's something here that has been missing in my life. Maybe that's why I have been avoiding dating relationships. Maybe Cody has figured out the secrets to this family thing."

What he was witnessing with Cody and his family was so different from his own experience, he wasn't quite sure if it was real or if the family was putting on a show for his sake.

Like the kids around the world that had difficulty sleeping that night, Ethan lay awake for several hours before finally drifting off to sleep with a smile on his face and more peace than he had felt in years. His insomnia and excitement was not caused by anticipation of presents to be received in the morning, but of the possibilities of a family life that he had never even considered to be available to him.

Chapter 27

New Year's Eve found Ethan driving into town to celebrate with the whole crew from Feathered Shaft. It was another one of Cody's traditions to bring the whole crew to *The Library*, a sports grill and brewery in Laramie. It was a tradition to celebrate the last season and to talk about plans for the new year and things that Cody wanted to add or change with FSO.

The wait staff had to combine several tables together to accommodate the dozen or so guides that worked for FSO. Sometimes, Cody would host all the family members of FSO, but tonight it was just the employees.

After they had all ordered, Ethan leaned back in his chair and looked around the table at all the guides who were engaged in spirited conversation with each other. The 2017 season had been a lot of work, but as he looked at each face, now cracking up and enjoying each other's company, he recalled the fun and adventures they had shared.

Memories came to mind of a first time fly fishing client and the excitement when they hooked into that first fish. The first fish caught on a dry fly is not easily forgotten.

He thought about the father and son from Omaha who had both taken elk. The excitement and joy was not at all diminished by the smaller-than-average antlers they were taking home. They were simply thrilled with the meat and the adventure they shared that would probably fuel memories for the rest of their lives. Even the game and fish that had gotten away were a key part of the adventures that they had been able to facilitate for the FSO clients.

Cody talked about these stories as he recounted all that had happened with the business that year. The admiration for Cody by every one of his employees was evident in their faces, laughing and ribbing each other when Cody would point out funny or embarrassing events from the year.

Cody was a master storyteller and, after forty-five minutes of his stories, Ethan's side and face were splitting from laughing so much. If he wasn't such a good outfitter, Ethan thought that Cody could be the best cowboy stand up comedian in the West.

When everyone got their food, Cody told the crew that he would finish up the meeting after everyone had a chance to eat. As everyone was finishing their meal, Cody raised his voice, "All right guys...can I get your attention again? 2017 was a great year, our best ever, actually. We had 20% more fishing clients and nearly 40% more hunting clients than we had in 2016.

"I want to continue with what we do well, but I think we need to expand in 2018. I will be looking for a few more guides for our normal trips, but I also wanted to let you guys know about an exciting new opportunity we have to expand. Some long-time clients have been hounding me for the last few years about offering some trips up in Alaska. They like FSO and want us to take them on an Alaskan adventure instead of hiring another outfitter there. I have been able to make some connections up there and I think we can maybe pull it off this year."

The excitement around the table was palpable. Even though all of the guides were experienced outdoorsmen, none had been to Alaska and Ethan could tell by the evident excitement on their faces, all of them wanted to be a part of this new adventure with FSO.

Later that night, as they all made their way out to the parking lot, Cody caught Ethan by his truck and asked "How was it for you tonight, being your first FSO New Year's meeting and all?"

"Yeah, it was good. Thanks so much for the food. They make a mean pizza," Ethan replied.

"Yep."

There was a long pause and Ethan could tell that Cody had more to say. He cleared his throat. "Hey, could you come to my house tomorrow? We need to talk about a few business details."

Ethan got to Cody's about 11:00 the next morning. Cody handed him a beer as he sat down at the kitchen table.

"No, thanks. I've had some issues in the past with alcohol."

Cody hesitated a bit before he spoke. He got a serious look on his face and his eyes got an intense look about them. He cleared his throat. "I respect that you know yourself and you don't want the temptation, but something tells me that you won't have an issue with that anymore.

"In the past, you drank to forget. Now, you can drink, not to get drunk, but to enjoy time with your friends."

Ethan was shocked. Nobody had ever spoken to him like that before. The way Cody talked sounded like a dad correcting his son. Ethan felt like Cody had the authority to speak things into being in his life. He knew that was weird. He wasn't sure why, but he felt like he could trust Cody with this as well.

He took the beer and decided that he would try it. He would only drink a beer with friends, never by himself. Somehow he knew that, if he did what Cody said, he wouldn't have an issue with substance abuse again.

While he pondered what Cody had just declared about him, he changed the subject. "Ok, what did you want to talk about?"

Chapter 28

"May 1, 2018," Ethan started a journal entry as he waited for his flight at Denver International Airport. The last several months had flown by. He couldn't believe that Cody had asked him to spearhead the Alaskan part of FSO's business.

He was the least experienced guide, but also had the least number of commitments in Wyoming. All the other guides had family or other work obligations in the off season so, on January 1, Cody had asked Ethan to go up to Alaska early in the spring. He wanted him to scout out places to hunt moose, caribou, and bears, both black and grizzly. This year, they wouldn't do any guided fishing trips, but Ethan was supposed to also find good salmon fishing for future trips.

"Not a bad job, getting paid to hunt and fish in Alaska," Ethan thought as he closed his journal and looked around the terminal at his gate. He liked to watch people when they weren't aware that they were being watched. Research and observation of humans in their natural habitat, he liked to call it.

One family caught his attention. They had a teenage son and two younger daughters, probably about ten and seven. The dad was using his phone for a video business meeting, talking loudly about some sort of real estate deal. The mom, taking several selfies and often interrupting the kids, all on their own devices, to get them to pose and smile for a picture.

Ethan imagined the social media posts about their amazing family vacation to the Colorado Rockies; how great it is to connect with nature, and do things together. The posts would, no doubt, include some cute saying like "be present" or "enjoy every minute with those you love."

Ironically, Ethan watched as each member of the family was lost in their own digital world, emerging only for the fake smile, for the fake post, about their fake family connection.

Perhaps he was judging too harshly. He didn't know this family. Maybe they were normally very attentive to each other and were not always "left to their own devices." He couldn't help comparing and contrasting them to Cody's family. They weren't perfect either, but they had an amazing family bond which was healthy, in Ethan's estimation at least.

He looked at this family again and figured that they were on their way home. The mom had on a purple sweatshirt with *"Washington Huskies"* in bold white letters across the front. The first leg of Ethan's journey gave him a two-hour layover in Seattle before the final leg to Fairbanks.

Thinking about the family, so lost in their own worlds, made Ethan wonder about this strange digital age. He thought about how much had changed, even since he was a kid. The kids across from him would never know what it's like not to have immediate access to unlimited information. He remembered having to look up information in books at a library. He missed those days. Was it just his imagination or was he able to retain what he learned better from words on paper compared to words on a screen?

These kids would never be able to appreciate a night sky with only natural lights in it; stars, planets, and moon. The number of satellites visible at night now was astounding and increasing all the time. Even when Ethan was in the wilderness for months, he couldn't enjoy the nighttime view without the "space junk," as he called it, outshining the stars in their slow movements across the sky. With a dark night and clear view, there was always at least one satellite in view at all times.

He wondered how much more technology society could handle. It's too much, too fast. Amazing inventions being used for both good and evil purposes. It was overwhelming when he allowed himself to dwell on it for very long.

Ethan's thoughts turned toward where he was headed. He hoped that there, technology would take a back seat to good old fashioned woodsmanship. He hoped that, in Alaska, life would slow down, like it had been in the backcountry for him after his elk hunt in Colorado.

His thoughts were interrupted when the intercom barked, "Group C, you may now board for your flight to Seattle, Washington. Thank you for choosing to fly with United today. Please have your tickets or phone confirmation ready for our staff at the gate and enjoy your flight."

Ethan shouldered his pack and walked toward the gate. He was excited, but a little apprehensive about this new adventure, wondering where it would take him and wondering if he was really cut out for all that Alaska could throw at him. He took one last look to the west at the mountains above the Denver skyline, remembered his time up there, and boarded the plane.

Chapter 29

When Ethan touched down in Fairbanks, he wasn't sure what to expect from the weather. He could see that it was sunny, but the biting wind when he stepped out of the terminal made him scramble for his jacket.

Naturally, it was on the very bottom of his pack. He drew some knowing smiles from the more sagacious Alaskans when they spotted his pile of belongings stacked on top of his suitcase. It took a few minutes until he could retrieve the camo jacket and repack, causing him to be more than a little self-conscious.

"First time to Fairbanks?" A young couple about the same age as Ethan stopped to welcome the greenhorn. The man continued, "I'm Mark and this is my wife, Leah. We saw you on our flight from Seattle."

"Ethan…nice to meet you." He paused long enough to shake their hands and then finished stuffing his belongings into his pack. "Yeah, first time. How could you tell?"

Mark laughed, well, you stand out a bit in that cowboy hat. Are you here on vacation? Ethan liked these two instantly. Mark was friendly and talkative. Leah hadn't yet spoken, but her face was as welcoming as Mark's words with an attentive gaze and quick smile.

"Not a vacation. I'm here for work, at least until October or November, probably."

"Ahh, cool. Welcome to Alaska. We actually have the afternoon free. Do you need a couple of tour guides to show you around town?"

"That would be amazing," Ethan answered. "I have a hotel room booked and my rental car is out in this parking lot somewhere, but I'm starving. Does this town have a sports bar or something where we can get a pizza and a beer?"

"*The Banks*," Leah's quiet voice seemed to match her personality and looks perfectly. "They've got great beer and pizza. We go there quite a bit when we're in town."

Ethan was mildly disappointed that his phone was able to pull up directions to the pub, but he was confident that he could find some spots away from Fairbanks where he could escape the cell signal. Anyway, he hoped he could find that off-grid Alaska that he had heard about.

"Just let me check into my hotel and I can meet you guys there in about forty-five minutes. I'm buying. That's the least I can do for a real live Alaskan tour of Fairbanks. You guys are real live Alaskans aren't you?"

Mark and Leah laughed and Mark answered, "I grew up here and Leah is a transplant from the lower forty-eight. She came as a freshman in high school, so she's nearly an Alaskan native now, just talks a little funny sometimes with her strange accent."

Mark feigned pain from the quick punch to his arm from Leah. "All right. See you over there in forty-five," Mark called over his shoulder as they walked out to their car. He was still pretending to be hurt, rubbing a large bicep that Leah would have a hard time hurting, no matter how hard she swung a fist. Ethan smiled, liking his new tour guides already.

The Banks Alehouse did not disappoint. The food, drink, and atmosphere were all great, but Ethan enjoyed the company even more. Mark and Leah introduced him to several of their friends who stopped by the table to say hi.

Ethan learned that Mark worked as a carpenter, mainly constructing log homes, and Leah was a substitute teacher. Their main passion however, was racing dog sleds.

They had both fallen in love with dogsledding and each other when they were in high school. They had built up their team now to about fifty adult dogs and ten puppies that they were training. "We hope to have both our teams ready to run the Iditarod next March," Mark confided. "We have enjoyed the small races, but the 'Last Great Race' is the dream.

"We'll see if we can get the money together. It's expensive. Tens of thousands to fly dogs and manage all the details of the race." Ethan had heard of the race, but he had never thought about how much it would cost to compete.

Ethan knew nothing about dogsledding, but he couldn't help getting sucked into their passion for the sport. The couple promised to take him out on their modified wheeled dogsleds once the mud season was over and the ground was solid enough to run the dogs.

Mark's face was animated as he spoke and Leah's was just as passionate when she talked about the dogs. "They always go crazy this time of year when they can't pull. They live for it. We can train with snow or solid ground, but we have to take a break for the mud."

Ethan could see the love that Mark and Leah had for the sport and their dogs as they talked about each one and their own individual personalities. "When I first moved here, I thought that dogsledding was cruel," Leah shared. "Now, I know that it would be cruel not to run these dogs. They are born for it. They would probably die if you tried to turn them into a house pet."

"All right. I think we've probably overloaded you with enough dogsled information," Mark interjected. "Tell us about you."

"No, it's fascinating," Ethan countered. "I love hearing about other people's passions. Me? Umm, I'm up here scouting for hunting and fishing opportunities for my boss. I work for an outfitter in Wyoming, but we are expanding into Alaska."

The conversation continued as Ethan paid for lunch and the couple drove him around the town. They didn't walk around too much because everything was either slush or mud. They were still wearing footwear appropriate for airplanes, but not for the Alaskan springtime.

By the end of the tour, Ethan was sure that he had a good idea of the layout of Fairbanks and that he had met its friendliest couple. Mark and Leah were about the same age as Ethan and were easy to talk to.

They had promised that they would check with a friend who owned a little cabin close to their place on the Chena River to ask if he would rent it to Ethan for the next six months.

As they dropped him off at his rental car back at *The Banks*, Leah piped up, "Hey did you notice our server Carly?"

Ethan looked to where she was pointing through the window of the restaurant where the waitress was writing down a food order on her notepad. Her shoulder length brown hair was streaked with a few dyed blonde strands.

Ethan found her attractive, especially the way she joked with them at the table with a very quick wit and dry sense of humor. He flushed. "Yeah?" he said slowly, more as a question than a statement.

"Well, I happen to know that she's single and I happened to notice she's into you."

"Leah?" Mark interrupted, saying her name slowly, also as a question.

Leah ignored Mark and kept going. "I could totally set you guys up. She's a sweet girl."

Mark stepped in again, mercifully. "Ahem," he coughed. "Well we've got about sixty mouths to feed when we get home. It's been great meeting you, Ethan. We'll have you over for dinner sometime next week, and I'll let you know what I find out about the rental cabin."

Ethan got out of the car and leaned on the open passenger window. "Sounds good, Mark and..." Ethan addressed Leah. "Thank you for looking out for my romantic interests, but I'm kinda off the market right now. I will make it a point, though, to be friendly with Carly next time I'm in there."

Leah beamed. "That's all I can ask. Who knows what can happen when one is friendly?" she said with a wink. They all laughed as Mark drove away and Ethan marveled at how quickly and easily he was becoming friends with the couple.

Chapter 30

Ethan's plan was to go right away up to the Yukon River to scout, but he heard that it was still iced up. He was quickly learning that all plans in Alaska are contingent on the weather. Trying to work against mother nature is futile here.

He spent the next few weeks working on details so that when the river opened up, he would be ready to utilize his time well. He wanted to really learn the land where he would be guiding clients and he was worried that with this setback, he would not have enough scouting time before the fall season when his clients would arrive.

He moved into the cabin that Mark and Leah had found for him. It was perfect. It was small, remote, secluded, but still not too far away from Fairbanks and Highway 2 that he would use to get up to the Yukon River.

With FSO money, he bought a truck, a boat, and boat trailer to use both for hunting as well as future fishing trips. The idea was to fly the clients into Fairbanks and then, using smaller planes, shuttle them on up to the Athabascan village of Fort Yukon.

From there, Ethan would meet up with the clients and take them upriver in the boat to a remote hunting camp. He had his backpacking gear that he would use for scouting, but Cody had already ordered wall tents and cots that were being shipped up from a canvas company in Montana to use during the hunts.

Ethan didn't bring any firearms to Alaska with him, but for bear protection, he knew he needed to carry some firepower here. After talking to several locals who had experience with Alaska interior grizzlies, he found a gun store in town and bought a shortened 12 gauge pump action shotgun, a .45-70 lever action, and a .44 Magnum revolver. Practicing with the firearms, he felt confident at close range, inside of thirty yards, but he hoped that this skill wouldn't have to be utilized out in the woods. Still, having the guns handy added a bit of courage and confidence as he was still a little unsure of himself in this novel environment.

After about three weeks, Ethan was having dinner with Mark and Leah, now a semi-common occurrence as he lived just a few miles up the road from their house. He was sharing some pronghorn steaks with them that he had asked Cody to ship up. The meat was from a doe that he had taken last year. He had shot it with his recurve at a water hole on the Wyoming prairie, quite a contrast to the spruce forest where he now found himself.

"This meat is amazing!" Mark gushed, suddenly very interested in hunting in Wyoming, especially after Ethan had shown Mark and Leah a video of his hunt. "Maybe you could teach me how to use one of those things," Mark said, pointing at Ethan's bow on the screen.

"Yeah for sure. You might want to get one that's a low poundage to start with, though." Before the night was through, two new recurves and two dozen arrows were ordered online for Mark and Leah. Ethan was happy to share his passion with them just as they had shared their love of dogsledding with him.

Mark had years of experience hunting with a rifle, but no one in his family had hunted with a bow, so he had never tried it. They usually would hunt moose and caribou every year for their winter meat, but with long-range rifles and scopes. It was less about the hunt and more about using the most efficient weapon to get their meat for the winter.

Leah had never been interested in hunting before, but she got excited about the possibility of using a bow to hunt. Ethan figured he would need to spend as much time teaching them the patience and ethics of hunting with the bow as he would spend on the mechanics of being a proficient shot with one. He was looking forward to the challenge.

Mark and Ethan went outside after dinner. After they had fed the dogs, they drank a beer around the fire pit. "Hey, we're really glad that we ran into you at the airport. It's just been a few weeks, but we really like hanging out with you and sharing our passions. Alaska can be a lonely place and it's sometimes hard to make friends.

Actually, I was feeling pretty down when we met you. A good friend of mine, Jason, took his own life and we were just flying back from his memorial service in Washington State when we met you at the airport.

Jason was out trapping this last winter and didn't come home when he was supposed to. His girlfriend had just broken up with him right before the trapping season started. He was pretty bummed about it, but I had no idea he would commit suicide.

When I hadn't heard from him in a couple of weeks, I went in with my dog sled team and found him at the cabin." Mark's eyes were red and his voice quavered, but he continued. "He figured I would come looking for him, so he left me a personal note."

Mark was silent for several minutes as he fought through his emotions thinking about that day. Ethan allowed the silence until Mark decided to break it. "Sorry. Didn't mean to put a damper on the evening, but I just wanted to say that meeting you at the airport felt like a setup. Like…God maybe was giving me back something that was stolen from me.

"You remind me a lot of Jason, actually. You guys would have hit it off. Anyway, I don't know why I told you all that."

Ethan felt Mark's pain. "No, you're good. I have my own stories of people I've lost. I'll tell you about 'em sometime." The two men shook hands when Ethan stood to leave. He felt like more was communicated in that handshake than the words that they had spoken.

When Ethan got to his cabin, he stoked the fire before climbing into bed. The nights were still cold enough for a fire at night, but every day was getting warmer as spring slowly, but inevitably, pushed winter back.

As he drifted off to sleep, he thought about what Mark had said. "Was there something or someone pulling the strings or…what did Mark say, giving back what was stolen or something?

He thought back over the last few years of his life. How had he gotten here from that confused, broken, depressed man in Colorado? He recalled the elk hunt, the long trek alone into Wyoming, the slim odds of Cody's guides finding him when he was nearly dead, the kindness of Cody and his unwarranted trust in him.

Now, here he was in Alaska, living a dream he hadn't even known that he had. He almost didn't recognize himself, he had changed so much. Maybe there was some deity causing things to go right for him.

He would have to talk it through with his journal tomorrow, but for now, with his window open to the clean Alaska air, he succumbed quickly to sleep.

Chapter 31

Ethan was finally on his way to the Yukon River. Highway 2 was proving to be challenging. He had narrowly missed two moose and a porcupine so far, and he was not quite halfway there.

He turned onto Highway 11 at Livengood, population thirteen. "I guess for those thirteen, it is livingood."

He joked to himself that maybe he should move up here, just to increase the population by nearly 10%, but he liked living near Fairbanks, in no small part due to Mark and Leah. Even though he had only known them for a month, he was going to miss them when he made his trips north.

During the summer, he was planning to come back to Fairbanks twice a month to resupply, but once the hunting season started, he would only have a few breaks to make it back. He was the sole guide this year, but if all went well, he would have more guides to help out next year.

When Ethan got to the Yukon River, he eyed it suspiciously. It was a big, strong river and he was unsure how the current would test his little boat and his limited river skills.

He relaxed a bit after traveling several miles upstream, but he told himself not to get two complacent. It looked like the river was angry and wouldn't be too forgiving of mistakes.

He stopped in Fort Yukon and stayed for several days, asking about what was upstream. He was trying to get information about game and fish in the area. Almost everyone in town were fishermen, trappers, or hunters who knew the area quite well.

He found the people there to be very friendly, but understandably reluctant to give him precise locations and numbers of animals. They were protective of the places where the best fishing and hunting was.

For many of these people, subsistence fishing and hunting in the summer and fall was a matter of survival in the winter. Telling too many people where to find the game could make it more difficult for them to use those areas themselves.

When Ethan indulged that FSO was only catering to bowhunters, several members of the community started to open up to him and gave him good intel on where to start. Ethan figured that they were skeptical that anyone could be successful hunting with just a bow, so they didn't feel threatened by the new outfitter in the area.

They also warned him about tricky areas on the river and where high populations of bears could steal meat and ruin your day. As he got information from the locals, he made notes on a map that he had printed in Fairbanks and made a mental note not to lose that map.

The first day from Fort Yukon, Ethan pushed up the river as far as he could. Sunlight lasted most of the night, but he finally pulled up to a sandbar at about 2:00 a.m.

He tied off the boat securely to a tree and pitched his tent right there on the sand. He went to sleep almost immediately, but was awakened three hours later by something sniffing around his head just outside the tent.

He slowly sat up and reached over to his .44 that, thankfully, he had remembered to set next to his sleeping pad a few hours before. The sniffing was moving around the tent and now he could see a distinct grizzly bear shadow on the side of the tent from the sunlight in the Northeast.

He partially unzipped the tent door very slowly, careful not to make sudden moves that would trigger the bear to attack. He could hear the bear breathing as it moved around the tent.

He reached out with the revolver, aimed at a nearby tree, and fired. His ears were ringing after the blast, so he didn't trust his hearing, but the shadow on the tent was gone.

He popped his head out of the tent just in time to see two grizzly cubs jump out of his boat and run right past the tent to get to their mom who was huffing and popping her teeth. She stood her ground until the cubs were safely past her into the brush.

Ethan noticed how shaky his hand was. It caused the barrel of the handgun to dance unsteadily and he wondered if he could pull off an accurate shot if he needed to. He continued to point the gun at the sow until she slowly turned to follow her offspring down the riverbank.

"This state is going to have to vet their employees a bit better. The Yukon River Welcoming Committee needs to work on their customer service skills a bit." Joking out loud about the bears working for the state of Alaska seemed to steady his nerves a little even though no one else was there to appreciate his humor.

A quick look around showed Ethan's mistakes from the night before. He had left most of his food in the boat in a cooler that the bears hadn't been able to get into. Muddy footprints on the lid and some claw and teeth marks indicated that they had tried. He had, however, left a bag of food in the boat that the cubs had torn into. He thought that losing a few candy bars and beef jerky was a small price to pay compared to how that could have gone.

Also, he now noticed a well-used bear trail right between his boat and tent. He was too tired last night to notice the trail, but promised himself not to be so careless in the future. "These inland grizzlies are a bit mischievous," he said as he replaced the spent casing in the revolver.

Ethan decided that further sleep here was improbable, so he packed up and decided to get an early start on the river. He had a spot on his map that he wanted to scout for moose. He figured that a ten-hour boat ride would probably get him there today and then he hoped to spend about two weeks looking the area over. He also hoped to not have too many bears in that area or it might be a long two weeks.

Chapter 32

Ethan did have another run in with a bear on his first trip. This time, it was a black bear. About one week into his scouting trip, he had his food bag hung up in a tree while he was away from camp. A smart black bear climbed the tree, scooted out onto a branch, and had bitten the rope holding the food bag which dropped it to the ground.

When Ethan arrived back at camp, he found the bear tearing into all of his remaining food. The bear was reluctant to leave even when Ethan got close to it and yelled at it. He threw a stick, hitting the bear in the side. At this, the bear growled, jumped up, straddled the food, and faced off with Ethan, unwilling to give up his dinner.

Ethan didn't want to shoot the bear, so he sprayed him in the face with bear spray, finally convincing him to vacate the camp. Between the bear and the spray, all of Ethan's food was totally ruined. He made a mental note to get some bear canisters for future trips.

Ethan had been finding some promising sign that the moose used this area during the fall season, but there were two other spots upriver that he wanted to check out before he left. On the map, one of the areas looked good for caribou, but he wanted to verify that there were well used trails indicating seasonal migration routes for the nomadic animals.

Packing up his camp to move, he pulled out a fishing rod to use enroute. Slowly trolling upriver, he caught two chinook salmon and a Dolly Varden on the way to his next camp. He figured he could survive on these three fish for the trip even if he didn't catch anything else.

He smoked the fish meat and then was able to arrow a snowshoe hare several days later. He now had plenty of food to finish his trip, but was definitely missing his coffee.

Several days before he was going to head back downriver, Ethan was introduced to Alaska's infamous fickle weather. The weather had been great for the whole trip up to this point, but a big storm blew in and the rain was torrential for days. Ethan huddled in his tent waiting for the storm to pass, but it seemed like she was an unwelcome guest who was happy to overstay her welcome.

With no way to get a weather forecast, he finally decided to brave the rain on the fourth day of the storm. He wrapped up his gear in a tarp, threw it in the boat, and steered the boat out into the current of the mighty Yukon.

The rain was causing the river to overflow its banks and the current was so fast that he nearly made it back to Fort Yukon by the end of the day. The storm clouds made it darker than usual, so by midnight, Ethan figured that he had better find a place to camp.

Several times, he had close calls with sweepers in the river. The high waters had uprooted trees which were getting tangled up together with other trees on the shore. This caused dangerous conditions for the small boat.

Ethan knew that if he got his boat tangled up in a sweeper it would be a serious, if not fatal, mistake. The darker conditions made it hard to see these deadly obstacles, especially if they were tangled up just around one of the thousands of tight corners on the river.

A few miles upriver from Fort Yukon, he beached his boat and drug it up the sandy bank quite a ways before tying it off so that the floodwaters couldn't take it downstream.

When he unpacked, he found that his sleeping bag had gotten soaked from the rain and water splashing over the sides of the boat all day. He decided to build a quick lean-to and use his rain fly as a roof, just as he had done in Wyoming. It took almost an hour to get a good fire going and he had to use some of the outboard fuel to ignite the wood and make it dry enough to burn.

Ethan had to work hard to keep the fire going all night so that he could stay warm enough. He didn't sleep at all and it seemed that the new day would never arrive.

Just as it was getting light enough to see, the storm broke and the sunrise was stunning. Even though he had been cold and miserable all night, Ethan was overwhelmed with the beauty and solitude of this place and he took time to savor the moment.

Just then, a bald eagle swooped down and caught a thirty inch salmon just as the morning sunlight hit its outstretched wings. Ethan watched it struggle to get the fish out of the water, but it finally made it over to the opposite bank. With his binos, he watched the majestic bird start to eat its breakfast before he wrestled his boat down to the water and pointed it downstream.

If he hurried, he might be able to get back to Fairbanks today. He wanted to stop in Fort Yukon and spend some time with his new Athabaskan friends there, but the thought of a hot shower and a warm bed tonight was too strong of a draw. He tipped his hat to the town as the current pushed him quickly past and he vowed to make time for a visit the next time he was here.

Chapter 33

Ethan made good time down the river to the El Patton Yukon River Bridge. He found a place to park his boat and trailer until his next trip when he could make it back to the river.

The drive back to Fairbanks was quicker without the trailer. As soon as he got cell service on his phone, he texted Mark. "Hey, I'm just getting back. Going to the store to stock up. Do you and Leah want to have dinner at my place tonight? Definitely my turn to host."

He made it to town and was halfway through his grocery list when his phone chimed.

"Yeah! Leah's running dogs and I'm working a bit late, setting rafters. 8 okay?"

Ethan responded and then circled back to pick up more steaks, potatoes, and corn on the cob. He was planning to start a big fire in his fire pit and cook everything outside. If he hurried home, he could get a good bed of coals going before Mark and Leah got there at 8:00.

While they enjoyed dinner together , the friends got caught up on what had happened over the last two weeks. Mark and Leah hadn't spent a lot of time up on the Yukon, so they were fascinated with Ethan's stories. He told them about the villages, life on the river, and the wildlife that he had encountered there.

Mark wondered out loud if it might work for him to go with Ethan next time he went up to scout, "I have a few weeks free after we finish the framing on the house we've got going over in North Pole."

Ethan was more than happy to have an extra set of hands in camp and to help scout for animals. They talked excitedly about the details for ten minutes before Mark turned to Leah.

"Would that be okay, babe? I don't have to go. The dogs are a lot of work for just one person."

Leah was relieved to see how excited Mark was for this trip. He had been pretty down since the day he had found Jason.

"No, you should totally go this summer before I get back to work in September. Maybe my coworker, Katie could come stay with me and help with the dogs. She's one of the teachers I substitute for. She's always asking me about the dogs and racing. Either way, you should go. I can manage the dogs for a couple weeks."

After dinner and s'mores, Ethan gave the couple an archery lesson with their new bows. He still wasn't used to the never-ending light in Fairbanks in the summer and they were still shooting at midnight when they finally called it quits and headed home.

Ethan knew that the couple would be up early in the morning to feed dogs before Mark left for work. He was happy that, in contrast, he could sleep in tomorrow. He was also happy that Mark could join him on his next trip north.

Before going to bed, he jotted down some things he needed to do before the next trip and wrote, "Call Cody tomorrow," at the bottom of the list. He knew Cody would be anxious to know what he had discovered so far. Cody was planning to fly up and join Ethan for his third trip up when he had discovered more about the terrain and animals there.

Chapter 34

The week in Fairbanks flew by for Ethan. He had found a couple of sixteen gallon steel drums that he decided to take up for food storage in his camps. He thought they would make good bear-proof containers.

He didn't want to repeat the mistakes from his last trip. Even the black bears that he had encountered here in Alaska seemed more aggressive and fearless compared to the bears he was used to in Colorado and Wyoming.

Mark's work required a few extra days than he had originally thought, but they finally got everything packed and started driving north up the road toward the Yukon. Both of the men were excited to share the adventure and camaraderie that they knew the next couple of weeks would bring.

When they arrived at the river, Ethan noticed that the water level was significantly lower than it was on his last trip.

"That should make it a bit faster to get up the river. We won't have to fight the current so much."

They had just gotten underway when Mark spotted a cow moose on the North bank.

"Alright!" he yelled back to Ethan from the front of the boat. The noise of the motor made it necessary to turn and yell to be heard. "I'm going to keep track of animal sightings. That's one for moose."

Ethan admired his friend's excitement as they sped by the moose. Mark held one finger in the air, showing it to the moose as if to tell her she was the first of the trip.

Two moose and one eagle later, they pulled into Fort Yukon at about 1:00 in the afternoon. They ate their lunch and talked to several of the elders there about what was upstream on the Upper Mouth.

On his last trip, Ethan had followed the main southern branch of the river, but he wanted to see what was on Yukon's northern branch from Fort Yukon.

They got some conflicting reports from the five or six older men who knew the area. Ethan concluded that they probably all remembered the river differently based on the last time they had hunted there. Most of them now relied on younger family members for their meat.

Two hours after pulling into town they were back on the water. All of the advice they had gotten in Fort Yukon warned about aggressive bears, but they didn't get much information about other animals. They would just have to find out for themselves.

They motored up river until about 8:00 in the evening when Ethan spotted a likely campsite on a gravel bar. They found numerous grizzly tracks however, so they continued for a few more miles. They made camp on an island that appeared to be less frequented by the bruins.

The night proved uneventful and the two men continued on upstream the next day into what looked to be good ground for caribou. They set up camp on the north side of the river because the ground to the north seemed to be best for the nomadic animals.

They had to move camp a few times before they found what looked to be the perfect place to ambush caribou with a bow. They had found where multiple trails had all converged into one trail between lakes.

The trail through a pinch point was several feet deep into the tundra where countless caribou had migrated through. The two men hypothesized that this trail had been used for perhaps hundreds of years.

They built a rock ground blind within twenty yards of the trail, much like native hunters had done for thousands of years in an effort to secure meat with a sharp arrow.

The blind was a difficult three mile hike through muskeg from their camp on the river, but Ethan was optimistic that the hunting here would be good if the caribou would cooperate. The animals were notorious for being unpredictable in their migration patterns year to year.

Ethan was happy with what they had found so far, but he wanted to push further upriver to see what the area held. They had four days before Mark needed to get back to work and Ethan wanted to get as much intel on the area as possible.

Ethan brought up the idea at dinner. "I want to run upriver another twenty miles tomorrow and see what we can find."

Mark replied, "Sounds good. I'm game for whatever, as long as I can shoot my bow."

They were eating a dinner of rice and a grouse that Mark had managed to arrow. He had brought his bow on the trip and was proving to be a quick learner hunting small game.

Snowshoe hares, squirrels, and grouse were not safe if Mark could get within about ten yards. The grouse that Mark had taken today was a welcome addition to the camp larder.

Ethan smiled as he knew what the obsession with traditional archery was all about. It was fun to experience it with a new bowhunter. Mark was like a kid at Christmas with his new passion. Ethan had uncharacteristically not hunted on this trip, just so that Mark would have more opportunities with his bow.

Before climbing into the tent for the night, they packed up most of the camp for an early departure in the morning. Ethan went quickly to sleep, but was awakened in the early morning to the sound of the tent zipper.

He saw Mark getting ready to exit the tent. "Hey! Take the shotgun," he whispered.

Mark responded by grabbing the gun. "Oh, yeah. I'll just be a minute to empty my bladder."

A few minutes later, a yell pierced the otherwise quiet forest. Fearing the worst, Ethan grabbed his .44 and headlamp and raced toward where he had heard Mark yell out.

"Mark! You okay? Where are you?" A few seconds of silence seemed like an eternity as Ethan waited for a reply.

"Over here!"

Now, Ethan could see Mark's headlamp through the willows. He was making his way back towards camp, but he had a noticeable limp.

"Did you run into a bear?"

Mark laughed, "No. I was looking out for bears, but I wasn't looking for porcupines. My eyes were scanning around and I wasn't watching where I was walking. I accidentally kicked porky and he didn't take too kindly to that. He swatted my leg with his tail and left me with a few gifts."

Ethan aimed his headlight beam onto Mark's lower leg and saw probably twenty quills in his boot and maybe a dozen more in his leg just above the boot line.

After Ethan extracted the quills with his Leatherman tool, the two friends shared a laugh about how they would have appeared if someone else had happened into the camp at that moment. Two heavily armed men, dressed only in boots and underwear would make for quite a sight.

"Well, I think this changes the plan," Ethan mused after the laughter subsided. "I forgot to grab my first aid kit out of the truck. Those quill wounds could get infected, so we better get you down to Fort Yukon tomorrow to get them cleaned out and sterilized.

"I need to make sure that I have my kit when I've got clients up here. Thanks for the entertainment and the reminder to have everything I need when I bring the clients in."

"My pleasure," Mark responded good-naturedly, "Here to serve."

Ethan knew that Mark was in pain, but he was also not a complainer. He was still light-hearted and having fun even when he was hurting, a rare quality that made Ethan appreciate his friendship with Mark even more.

He knew that they would remember this trip, and hopefully many more, with fond memories in the future. Before they got back to Fairbanks, Mark had come up with a hilarious story about the incident. He called it the *Underwear Attack of the Killer Porcupine*, which included quite a few embellishments to complement what had really happened.

Chapter 35

Ethan met Cody at the Fairbanks airport, excited to show him all that he had found on his trips north. He took him to The Banks for lunch and then on to his little cabin where he was staying. They would leave in the morning, but they loaded up the truck with gear so that they could get an early start.

Canvas wall tents, cots, portable wood stoves, cooking stoves, fuel –the list was extensive. The truck, and later the boat, would be well-loaded.

The friends got caught up on the three hour drive to the river. Ethan asked Cody about his family.

"Oh, that reminds me. The kids sent you a birthday present. They all pooled their money and got you this." Cody pulled a custom skinning knife from his coat pocket. Ethan took the knife and held it up. The blade was sheathed, but he could see that the handle was made of antler and there was a bull elk carved into it.

While driving, it was difficult to fully appreciate the knife, but the emotions that the gesture evoked in Ethan quickly filled his heart with gratitude for his adopted Wyoming family. "Tell them…" The rest of the sentence caught in his throat.

After several seconds, Cody placed a hand on his shoulder, "I will," he said quietly. "The kids will be glad you like it."

The men were quiet for 30 minutes before Ethan broke the silence, "So, how does it look for hunts this fall? Who has booked a hunt?"

The rest of the drive they talked about business, both here in Alaska and back in Wyoming.

They got an early enough start that they were able to make it all the way to Camp One by evening. Camp One was in a spot that Ethan hoped would provide good moose hunting. It was located on the southern fork of the river.

Camp One was a good location for bears, but he had also found a spot that he called "Bear Canyon," which had an even greater population of bears, both black and grizzly. Bear Canyon would be a spike camp, south of Camp One, about five miles overland.

Ethan figured that if a client was specifically looking for a backpacking grizzly hunt, they would utilize Bear Canyon for that. There was a tributary of the river that ran through Bear Canyon that Ethan hoped had a good salmon run in the fall, bringing in the bears.

When they pulled into Camp One, they went to work quickly setting up one of the wall tents in an area that Ethan had earlier cleared and leveled for that purpose. As summer was winding down, darkness came earlier. They finished setting up the tent in the dark at about 11:00. Both were worn out from the long day and were soon asleep.

Their 5:00 alarm was the grunt of a young bull moose who was slowly walking through the camp, seemingly curious about the new canvas structure along his normal route.

"Well, I think you may have picked a good spot, Ethan," Cody whispered as they watched the bull, through the open flap of the tent, move unhurriedly down the trail.

"Appears so. How about some coffee?" Ethan responded as he lit the stove.

They spent the rest of the day getting the camp set up. First, they erected the small cook tent, complete with four camp chairs, a plastic folding table, and a propane stove with two tanks of propane. Cody rigged up solar panels and batteries to run both the LED string lights for both of the tents as well as the all-important electric bear fence that they installed around the tents.

Building a fire ring and a sturdy meat pole completed Camp One. They spent a second night in camp before moving on to their next spot.

Before leaving, they made sure that the fence was working and then jumped in the boat, pointing it downstream toward the confluence at Fort Yukon. Once there, Ethan pointed the boat upstream into the upper mouth.

It took all day to get to the spot he was calling Camp Two. They followed the same procedure and had camp pretty well set up and ready for clients by the end of day four.

Cody had to be back in Fairbanks to catch his plane in a few days, but on morning five of their trip, they figured they had enough time to hike into "Caribou Alley" before they had to leave. Caribou Alley was the name that Ethan picked out to call the spot north of camp where he had set up the rock blind.

As they came into view of the trail and blind, they noticed a group of five bull caribou coming off a distant hill. Cody and Ethan sat down on the tundra and watched the animals through their binoculars. As if on cue, the group funneled down the trail, right by the blind.

"That should work!" Cody stated the obvious. They hiked quickly back to camp so that they would have time for a quick stop in Fort Yukon on their way back downriver.

Ethan was quickly learning about native Alaskan culture and he knew that having Cody there to meet the elders would be honoring for them. He also wanted to show that they wanted to work with, not against, them in this outfitting venture.

He was learning that gaining trust from the entire community starts with the elders and that it took time and honor to gain their trust. Listening to their stories and following their advice had gone a long way for Ethan so far, but he knew that a lot more time was required to win their complete confidence.

It took patience, but it was not a hardship for him since he was really enjoying learning about the culture from those who had been thriving in this harsh landscape for generations.

Chapter 36

After Cody returned to Wyoming, Ethan was able to take two more trips north to his base camps. He did more scouting and exploring and felt pretty good about the upcoming hunts. He was confident that he could get his clients within bow range of animals, but the hunter's shooting skills, the weather, and how the animals themselves behaved were the wildcards on any hunt.

The goal for him was always about the adventure. Ethan tried to always emphasize the experience for the client so that they would feel like they got their money's worth, even if they were unsuccessful with the animals.

The last week of August, Cody returned to help guide as Ethan had 3 clients for his first trip. Cody needed to be back in Wyoming for a pronghorn hunt, but he had several days to help out in Alaska.

They met the clients in Fort Yukon as they got off the plane. After introductions, they shared a meal with one of the Athabaskan families that Ethan had met there.

He wanted to help with the local economy, so he paid a family to prepare a lunch for the hunters and then they gave a short history of the native way of life and their culture. This was an idea that he and Cody had discussed after his visit that seemed to be a win-win for both the local families and FSO.

The family members were happy that the hunters were interested in their culture and they were proud to talk about their heritage. It was an interesting bonus for the clients adding to the adventure of the hunt.

Ethan's first clients were a father-daughter from Missouri named Robert and Megan and an electrician, Joey, from Denver. This trip was a high school graduation present for Megan while Joey was intent on getting high quality video of his hunts for his YouTube channel.

All three had moose tags, and Joey also had a tag for grizzly bear. They started out at Camp One. Cody took Robert and Megan out around camp for several days to hunt moose while Ethan and Joey concentrated on bears, backpacking into Bear Canyon.

Day three was eventful for both groups as two animals were taken. Cody called in a beautiful bull moose for Robert and Megan.

Robert passed up an easy shot on the bull, so that it would move past him to his daughter. Robert was at full draw as the bull stepped into a clearing in the willows at only five yards. Even though Megan was set up just fifteen yards behind and to the left of her dad, she couldn't yet see the bull because of the thick brush. The bull was moving to the left, so Robert didn't shoot, hoping Megan would have a shot opportunity.

The bull cooperated and stepped out into a small clearing just seventeen yards in front of Megan. The enormous size of the animal shocked her, but she was able to keep her cool and executed a textbook double-lung shot. The bull only made it fifty yards into the willows before going down for good.

"Mom would be so proud," Robert said to his daughter as they stood over the animal. Cody learned that Robert's wife had been a bowhunter and had always wanted to hunt moose in Alaska.

Nineteen years earlier, Robert and his wife had made plans to do a moose hunt as a young couple. Only a positive pregnancy test and worries about future finances with a baby on the way had thwarted those plans.

"She said that we could do this hunt after Megan graduated," Robert explained to Cody while fighting back tears. "She lost her fight with cancer a year too soon."

Megan took up the story as her dad was too emotional to continue. "When Mom died, I started shooting her bow. I was never interested in it before, but now…it really connects me to Mom, you know?"

Now, it was Megan's turn to be overcome with emotion and Cody gave them time and space with the bull, father and daughter, connecting in a deeper way than they ever had before. The normal feelings of elation tinged with a level of sadness and sobriety that accompanied most hunts was compounded as the realization set in that the daughter had just accomplished her mother's goal.

Meanwhile, several miles away, Ethan and Joey had found a big interior grizzly bear that Joey was attempting to stalk. Ethan was doing his best trying to both film the hunt with Joey's camera and covering him with a lever action .45-70 rifle in case of a charge.

When they first spotted the bear, it was nearly a mile away, but they were now about seventy yards from the bear, who was busy digging for rodents and didn't notice their approach. When they got to within fifty yards, Ethan noted that the wind was still good. They were directly downwind and it was consistent, but he knew that it could change quickly as the day warmed up and started blowing uphill toward their quarry.

"Move in quickly when its head is down. I'll stay here while you close the distance."

Ethan set up the tripod and pushed the record button as Joey snuck in closer and closer. When the bear would look around, he would freeze, but then would move forward five or ten yards when the big bruin would start digging again.

Ethan estimated that Joey was about twenty-five yards from the bear when he knelt just to the right of a bush and got ready to draw his bow. The bear was facing directly away, so Joey had to wait.

About ten minutes went by and Ethan could see Joey's arrow bouncing around a little as the intensity of the situation was causing his bow arm to shake uncontrollably. Ethan hoped that Joey could hold it together if he got a shot.

Suddenly, a small gust of wind hit the back of Ethan's neck and the bear's head instantly came up out of the hole he was excavating. It looked like the bear just got a small whiff of the hunters, but he still didn't like it.

As he turned to run, simultaneously, Joey drew his bow and Ethan blew on a predator call. The bear hesitated just long enough for Joey to execute a perfect shot, his arrow zipping through the bear and ricocheting off a rock and into the bushes beyond.

The bear was confused about where the danger had come from since the arrow had made a loud crack behind him as it hit the rock. In seconds, he was running straight toward the hunters. Ethan aimed at the bear with the rifle, his finger tightening on the trigger, but held off as the bear veered slightly to the right and passed them, just four yards from Joey.

It entered a willow thicket and the two men could hear it thrashing around for several seconds before all was quiet. Ethan turned to see his hunter wide-eyed and now shaking uncontrollably.

"Dude! What the...? Did you see that? Is the camera...? You get that? Dude! Never in my life..." Ethan just grinned as Joey's inability to form a sentence revealed his level of excitement.

They waited a full hour before venturing into the thick brush to find Joey's bear, even though Ethan was positive that he had expired within seconds of the shot. They reviewed the footage while they waited and it revealed what both men had thought they had seen, a perfect shot through the big bear's chest and then the camera had captured most of the chaos that had followed the shot.

Both animals took another day to pack to Camp One. By then, it was time for Cody to head home, so Ethan left the three clients in camp while he transported Cody and the meat back to Fort Yukon. He dropped Cody off at the airport and got the meat to the freezer of a local butcher shop in town.

When he returned to camp, he could tell by the look on Robert's face that their time alone in camp had been eventful. A bold black bear had tried to get into Megan's moose head and Joey's bear hide that were hanging on the meat rack. Robert finally got it to leave by hitting it in the face with bear spray.

Ethan thought that the spray would be enough to discourage it from returning, but he still strung up another electric bear fence around the head and hide. He wanted all the bears in the area to learn that there was no free food in his camp.

The remainder of the hunt was exciting as both Robert and Joey attempted to fill their moose tags. In the end, neither one was able to get a shot. They both had several close encounters with bulls, but something would always go wrong for the hunters and right for the moose.

Neither man was disappointed though. They both told Ethan that it had been an incredible adventure and that they wanted to come back next year.

Robert took with him an unforgettable adventure with his daughter that both of them would cherish for the rest of their lives. Joey was as excited about the footage he was bringing home as the trophy bear he had taken with his bow. He promised to highlight FSO when he posted his video on his YouTube channel.

The night before they left, four new friends celebrated their adventure in camp roasting marshmallows for s'mores over the dying embers of their last campfire for this trip in the far north.

Chapter 37

The boat ride back to Fort Yukon was cold as a light drizzle wet down gear and passenger alike. By looking at the hunter's faces, Ethan couldn't tell that conditions were miserable.

They all showed huge smiles revealing that even though Alaska was saying farewell with less-than-perfect weather, nothing could dampen the thrill of the adventure for these three. He opened up the throttle a bit more to add to the experience.

Getting close to Fort Yukon, Ethan cut back on the throttle, mainly just allowing the current to finish the trip. All were content but quiet, realizing that their adventure in Alaska was nearly over.

The mood on the boat changed instantly as they heard loud shouts coming from one of the houses located on the bank of the river. As they drifted by, Ethan could see a teenage boy with a shotgun on the porch of the house.

Several other people were there with the boy, trying to talk to him. Ethan could tell that the boy wasn't being threatening to the others, but instead had the muzzle of the gun trained on his own head, his thumb on the trigger, the gun's butt on the deck boards.

Ethan cut the engine and glided the boat into a dock just downstream and out of sight from the house.

"You guys stay here. I have an idea." He grabbed his bow and trotted between houses, cars, and snow machines to close the distance toward the drama that was playing out on the porch.

As he drew closer to the house, his senses on high alert, he heard a noise behind him. Glancing back quickly, he noticed Joey was following him and motioned for him to be quiet.

Joey nodded, worked his way to the left, and got behind a fifty-five gallon steel barrel. Joey could now see the porch and he motioned to Ethan that the boy was looking away, distracted by the others on the porch.

Peeking around the corner of a building, Ethan saw that the porch was about sixty feet away and that the boy had put the barrel of the gun into his mouth. He couldn't hear what the adults were saying to the young man, but he could tell that he was listening to them.

One rubber-tipped blunt arrow, usually used for small game, was in Ethan's quiver. He was going to try to shoot that arrow at the gun. He knew that, if he didn't time this right, his shot could cause the startled boy to flinch and pull the trigger. He braced himself for the most important shot of his life.

Someone must have asked the boy a question. As the barrel came out of the boy's mouth and tipped slightly forward, Ethan drew a breath and drew his bow.

The flight of the arrow only took a third of a second, but it seemed an eternity to Ethan. His eyes followed his fletchings for every rotation of the shaft, seemingly in slow motion, as it rose above the target mid-flight and then dropped back down.

The impact of the heavy arrow striking the stock of the gun achieved the desired result. The barrel was forced to the side and the startled teen flinched and squeezed the trigger. The deadly buckshot was harmlessly expended into the overhanging roof.

Before he could recover and rack another shell into the chamber, two men rushed forward. One secured the weapon while the other jumped on the boy to restrain him.

Thirty seconds later, a police officer arrived on the scene and took the boy into custody. As Ethan approached the house, the boy looked directly into his eyes.

He was on his stomach with his hands cuffed behind his back. The officer was keeping a knee on his back and writing details on a notepad while he asked the others what had happened.

The boy, who Ethan guessed was about fifteen, didn't say a word as Ethan approached, but his eyes spoke of hurt, sadness, and maybe a hint of relief that his attempt to kill himself was unsuccessful.

After the officer left to take him to the hospital for a psych evaluation, Ethan talked to one of the men who had been on the porch and had grabbed the gun from the boy.

"That was quite a shot," He said as he handed Ethan his arrow. "Anthony's my nephew, my brother's boy. I've been helping raise him since my brother died nearly two years ago."

"I'm sorry for your loss. What happened?"

"My brother was running his snow machine on the river, collecting his traps at the end of the season. There must have been a soft spot on the ice. We found the hole, but the machine and my brother were gone.

"Anthony was supposed to be with him collecting traps, but he had a test in school that day. He thinks he might have been able to save his father if he was there, but I've told him he probably would have just drowned with him.

"He's had a tough two years. He wants to do outdoor stuff like he did with his dad, but I'm a mechanic, not really an outdoorsman.

"I mainly work on boats, ATVs, snow machines, occasionally cars. My brother was the outdoorsman, but I don't really have time to take Anthony out in the woods much."

Ethan noticed that Joey had moved in close and was listening to Anthony's uncle as well and he was suddenly reminded that he needed to get his clients to the airport before they missed their flight.

They walked quickly back to the boat in silence, not wanting to think about what might have happened if Ethan's arrow had missed.

"Hey! What happened?", Megan asked Ethan when they met the father and daughter back at the boat. "We heard a gunshot!"

"Everybody's okay. I'll let Joey fill you in later on what happened. Right now, we need to get you guys downriver just a bit more to where my friend is waiting with his truck to get you to the airport."

A few minutes later, Ethan was saying goodbye to his first clients of the season before they were taken to the airport. After they left, his nerves were still on edge from the incident on the porch.

Ethan had two days to spend in town before the next clients arrived. He was planning to use the time to get supplies lined up for the next hunt, but first, he wanted to meet the boy from the porch.

Chapter 38

Anthony had been taken to the Yukon Flats Health Center where a mental health professional had given him an evaluation. Ethan asked at the front desk if he could see the boy, since he had been on scene with him. The nurse wanted to help, but she explained firmly that only the family was allowed to visit the patients.

As Ethan was leaving the hospital, Anthony's uncle arrived at the small clinic. Ethan explained what the nurse had said and Anthony's uncle simply said, "Wait here," with a grim look of determination.

In two minutes, he returned outside. "Let's go." As Ethan followed the man back inside, the same nurse sheepishly swiped her badge to unlock the door leading to the patient rooms.

Ethan noticed that all of the staff treated Anthony's uncle with honor, bowing slightly and lowering their eyes as he walked past.

"I'm sorry…who are you?" Ethan asked.

"My name is Jonny Yupik."

"And you said you're a mechanic?"

"Yes…Also, I am a tribal elder."

"Ahh, okay." Ethan realized that the respect for elders in native culture ran very deep in Alaska.

When they got to Anthony's room, Jonny didn't speak, but simply looked at the nurse who was sitting in the room. She got up and left the room, leaving them alone with Anthony.

Ethan stood near the door, feeling like an intruder as Jonny stepped up to the bed.

Several seconds of silence followed as nephew and Uncle communicated solely with their eyes. Anthony was the first to speak. "Uncle…I'm sorry, I…"

"It's okay Tony. I know." More silence. Anthony closed his eyes, his head leaned back on his pillow.

When he opened them again, he noticed Ethan, seemingly for the first time. "Hey, you're the…Robin Hood," repeating the name of the only archer he knew.

Ethan smiled warmly. "My name is Ethan." They shook hands.

"I've never seen anybody shoot a bow like that. Can you teach me?"

"Well, it seems you're on a seventy-two hour hold," Ethan said, recalling information that the front nurse had given him earlier. "I have to take some clients out hunting before you get out of here, but in about two weeks, I'll be back in town and we can shoot."

The boy's face exploded in a huge smile, making Ethan doubt his memory of what had happened on the porch only hours before.

Anthony was obviously impressed with Ethan's prowess with a bow, but he was doubly impressed when he found out that he had taken big game with the seemingly diminutive weapon. He had only been exposed to rifle hunting and was fascinated with the bow. He asked Ethan question after question about bow hunting, fishing, and anything related to outdoor adventure.

After about thirty minutes, Jonny interrupted the two. "Well, we need to go. I was told that they are going to do some therapy with you, Tony. It's kind of like a class. It starts in ten minutes. Tony, honor your teacher as you would your father or me."

Ethan marveled that this young man, obviously distraught and suicidal, still listened intently to his uncle.

"Yes, sir. I will." Anthony then turned to Ethan. "Thank you, sir."

"You're welcome." Ethan wasn't sure whether Anthony was thanking him for the visit now or for him stopping him on the porch, but he decided that Anthony would probably want to forget about the porch incident, so he didn't ask.

After they were outside, Jonny turned to Ethan. "You hungry? I think I owe you lunch."

"You don't owe me anything, but I am hungry. Would love to have lunch with you."

Over lunch, Jonny explained to Ethan about the suicide epidemic that was rampant in Alaskan native villages, especially among young people. Ethan could sense uncharacteristic emotions from the stoic man as Jonny told him about the problem. "Three people in my family have killed themselves, including Anthony's mom."

"She was so depressed after my brother died, she could barely take care of Anthony. One night, about five months after my brother's accident, someone saw her walk into the river that had taken him and they saw her just get swept downstream.

"They found her body five miles down river, caught in a log sweeper. The autopsy revealed that she had a lot of drugs and alcohol in her system.

"Anthony was devastated, but he's been doing better lately, until today. This morning, he just got the news that one of his friends from grade school, who had moved downriver to Nulato, just OD'd on fentanyl. It wasn't clear whether it was on purpose or an accidental overdose."

Jonny continued, "When I was a kid, we didn't have this problem. Everybody worked, hunted, and fished to live. We had purpose. Now, the government gives us money and food. Nobody knows the old ways. They tried to help us, but now, we have no purpose. Kids aren't motivated to do anything. Everyone wants the handouts, but the handouts are killing us."

While listening to Jonny, an idea came to Ethan. "I want to help Anthony if I can. He seems to love the outdoors. What if he became my apprentice? I could teach him outdoor skills, and pay him a little bit for his work. I could really use some help around camp, splitting firewood, cooking, keeping an eye out for bears. I'll have to run it by my boss, but what do you think?"

Jonny couldn't believe that Ethan would want to help his nephew like this. "Are you sure? Anthony can be kind of stubborn sometimes. He can be a handful. Losing both of his parents has been very tough and he sometimes doesn't know what to do with the grief."

Ethan considered carefully before answering, "I think I can handle him. He's had it rough and that stuff might come up and cause issues, but I'm up for a challenge.

Don't tell him yet. Let me check with my boss, we'll see how he does the next few days with mental health, and then I'll ask him before I take out my next clients. If everything works out, I could maybe take him to camp in a couple weeks."

"Thank you. I think Tony's life might have just changed." Jonny's voice shook with emotion and Ethan marveled at this proud native Alaskan. He commanded such respect and yet was unashamed to show humility and gratitude so openly with someone he had just met this morning.

That afternoon, as Ethan stocked up for his next hunt, he made the call to Cody and explained the situation. Ethan knew that Cody had a big heart for people who were hurting. He wasn't surprised when Cody welcomed the chance to give back to the Alaskan community. He told Ethan that FSO would pay for Anthony's wages and anything else Ethan needed for his mentorship.

Two days later, Ethan's next clients flew into Fort Yukon. He met them and took them out to Camp Two. Over the next ten days they had a great hunt chasing caribou.

Two of the clients were successful taking bulls and the third ended up wanting to spend more time fishing and hunting for spruce grouse than hunting for caribou. He, unsurprisingly, didn't get a caribou, but was happy with the fishing and small game hunting.

Ethan was intent on being an excellent guide, but his thoughts kept turning back to Anthony and what he had learned about the current plight of the Athabaskan people. Ethan wanted to help, but he knew the problems were complex and solutions would be difficult.

How do you help a proud people without being patronizing when too much help is a big part of the problem? He wasn't sure, but he was sure he could at least help Anthony if he was as enthusiastic about the outdoors as he seemed to be.

Chapter 39

When Ethan made it back to Fort Yukon, he found that Anthony had done well and was ready to turn his life around. Jonny told Ethan that Anthony seemed motivated and excited with the opportunity to work with him on his hunts.

Under the circumstances, Anthony's teachers were more than happy to work with him, giving him lessons to work on in camp so that he could keep up with his classmates. Anthony's schoolwork had suffered from the depression that plagued him, but now, he seemed eager to improve himself in that department as well.

As promised, Ethan taught Anthony about archery and he proved to be a quick learner when it involved doing anything with his hands. He gave him a bow and a dozen arrows that he had ordered for him as pre-payment for some of his work at camp. Before they left for camp, Ethan was confident that the grouse in the backcountry would not be safe from Anthony's arrows.

Anthony would be joining FSO for the last hunt of the season. Ethan wanted to spend more time with Anthony, but at least this would give him a taste for what outfitting was like. If things went well, it was something to look forward to for next year, starting with summer fishing trips.

They picked up the clients who would be on a ten day adventure in the Alaskan backcountry and introduced them to Fort Yukon. Anthony was shy when talking to the group, but he gave the clients a unique perspective about living in rural Alaska and they asked him many questions about himself and Athabascan culture. Ethan could see a new sense of pride come over Anthony as these strangers expressed interest in his people and customs and he was able to represent native Alaskans proudly.

As Ethan motored the boat upstream, he could tell that this would be a good trip. Everyone, including Anthony, wore wide smiles and were taking in all the sites, sounds, and smells that were unique to the Yukon.

At one point, Ethan cut the motor and drifted for a few minutes while the group watched three bald eagles feasting on fish on the opposite bank. While they watched, an osprey dove into the water and came up with a fish bigger than himself.

All the way to camp, each person pointed out fascinating things that they were seeing which made the experience that much more enjoyable for everyone. It was one of those perfect fall days in Alaska.

They made it to camp by mid-afternoon. Once their gear was in the tents, an archery tournament broke out in camp with everyone taking turns picking the next target. A pine cone at twenty-seven yards or a blade of grass at twenty-two were assaulted by feathered shafts until it was too dark to see.

That night Ethan and Anthony cooked moose steaks over hot campfire coals to round out a perfect day. Anticipation ran high for the start of the hunt tomorrow morning.

By day four, Anthony had fallen into the routine of camp life and was loving it. He and Ethan made breakfast together before Ethan took out the hunters. Then, Anthony would do camp chores; washing up after breakfast, chopping wood, prepping ingredients for sandwiches for lunch, and always keeping an eye out for pesky bears.

In the afternoons, Anthony was free to hunt with the bow that Ethan had given him. He had a blast and was often able to add a squirrel, grouse, or snowshoe hare to the larder and add interest to the meals.

Several days into the hunt, a brazen black bear wandered into camp at lunch time. One of the hunters wanted to go after the bear, but by the time he got out of the cook tent and got his bow ready, the bear had moved off about a hundred yards out of camp. Ethan called it back in with a squeaking sound that he made with his mouth. His client was able to take the bear at twenty yards.

Ethan was pleased, both that the client was happy with the bear, and that they had taken it out of the area. He was pretty sure that this bear had been responsible for many problems in camp this season.

They celebrated with some bear stew that night, cooked in a cast iron Dutch oven. Anthony was turning into quite the camp cook.

Before they knew it, the ten day hunt was over. Anthony was surprised and not a little disappointed that the time was gone and they were headed back to Fort Yukon. The boat was riding low in the water with all the meat from two moose, a caribou, and the black bear.

While the load was heavy, the mood was light as the group reminisced about the amazing adventure they had shared. They were tired, but very content and everyone felt that, somehow, time moved at a slower pace on such an adventure compared to the normal routine at home.

Soon the clients were on their way home in an airplane and Ethan and Anthony met Jonny at his house.

Over dinner, Ethan asked, "Hey, I've got to go back up to both camps and tear down for the season. Do you think you could spare Anthony for another week? I sure could use the help."

Johnny glanced at Anthony. He knew the answer, but asked anyway, "Do you want to go back up for another week?" Anthony nodded emphatically.

"Okay, if you check in at school and see if they're good with it, you can go." Anthony raced off without another word to catch his teachers before school let out for the day.

The two men used the time while he was gone to talk about how it was going with Anthony at camp. Both were pleasantly surprised with how well he was doing and how quickly he was learning outdoor skills.

"The healing power of nature is mysterious and without equal," Jonny remarked as they sat on the same porch where Anthony had nearly ended his life just a few weeks ago.

Each absorbed in their own thoughts, they listened to the crickets and the river as it endlessly followed gravity toward the sea.

Chapter 40

A few days later, Ethan and Anthony pulled the boat up to Camp One. Anthony jumped out and tied the bow of the boat to a sturdy tree. They threw their packs onto the cots in one of the wall tents and Anthony rubbed his hands together, eager to get to work.

"Where do you want me to start? Should I pack up the other tent?"

Ethan smiled. "Actually, I have a surprise for you. Your uncle and I got you a moose tag, so you're actually going hunting first before we clean up the camps."

"No way! No way! What the…Wait. My bow isn't strong enough for moose. I didn't bring a rifle."

"Your uncle thought of that. Your dad's rifle is in the boat. Go get it."

Anthony raced to the boat and found the gun. It was in its wolverine skin case and then wrapped in a tarp for protection and to keep it dry on the boat ride in.

Anthony brought it back to the tent. His hands were shaking when he took the gun out of its case. It hadn't seen the light of day in two years; since his dad had died.

They both admired the old Thompson Center single-shot break action Contender rifle, chambered in .30-06. It was no doubt picked for the versatility of the available ammo when it was new in 1980.

Anthony shared the story that he had heard his dad tell so many times. "He saved up his fur money for several years and was so proud when he could finally buy that rifle.

"He used to tell me, 'one shot, son. That's all you need. When you hunt, it's not so important to shoot accurately at long range when you are a good enough hunter to sneak into short range and kill your animal with one shot. One day, you will hunt with this rifle. Become a hunter that only needs one shot.'"

Ethan noticed that the rifle didn't have a scope. The iron sights testified that the man believed what he had told his son.

Anthony spotted a smudge on the side of the metal plate of the stock when he was admiring the rifle. A fingerprint. He pointed it out to Ethan who agreed that it must be his dad's from the last time he had cleaned it.

"Usually, he was really good about wiping his rifle down, but…I'm glad he missed that spot."

"I'm going to just step outside for a minute," Ethan said, to give the boy some time alone with the memory and fingerprint of his dad.

Five minutes later, when he stepped back into the tent, Ethan could see the tear streaks on Anthony's face. The teenager was as comfortable showing his emotions as his uncle was. Ethan felt a dull pain in his chest as the boy's grief reminded him of his own, losing his own father also when he was young.

"Do you want to use it?" Ethan asked, pointing to the gun. "I also have the .45-70 that you could hunt with if you would rather not use your dad's rifle."

Anthony took several minutes to think through the question. A part of him wanted to return the gun to the case to keep his dad's memory from mixing with other memories he would make hunting with it.

Finally, he replied. "I want to use it. Dad would want that." They took pictures of the fingerprint before it got rubbed off so that Anthony could later see the photos and remember. With a serious and determined look, he looked up at Ethan from where he sat on the cot. "Let's go find a moose!"

It took three hard days of hunting, but they finally found a bull that was responsive to calls. Anthony was not going to be picky for his first moose hunt, but Ethan realized, as the bull closed the distance through the willows, that this was the biggest moose he had seen all season. He was calling from behind and to the side of Anthony, hoping to pull the bull through a small opening in front of the hunter.

Ethan remembered to pull out his phone and he videoed the last twenty yards of the bull weaving his big antlers through the brush. He was grunting loudly as he stepped into the clear just thirty yards from the kneeling hunter.

Anthony held his breath and slowly squeezed the trigger. "This is for you, Dad," he whispered. "I love you."

At the report of the rifle, the confused bull ran straight at Anthony, stopping just five yards in front of and towering over the boy, who was still kneeling. For ten seconds, the bull and the boy stared at each other.

Anthony felt he was looking into the soul of his father through the eyes of the moose. When it fell forward, almost on top of Anthony, the weight of the bull hitting the ground was like an earthquake. He could feel the impact through his knees and it shook him to his core.

He reverently approached the dead moose. He took off his hat, covered the bullet hole with it, and thanked the animal for giving his life to feed his family, just as he had seen his father do when they had hunted together many years before.

Ethan could feel the solemnity of the moment for Anthony. He gave him time and space to take it all in. It seemed like Anthony was making peace with his father's death by experiencing the death of this magnificent animal taken with his father's rifle.

When Ethan approached, he asked if Anthony wanted him to take his picture to remember the hunt.

"I don't think so. My father never did, so I don't want to. I just want to take the antlers back to show my uncle."

It took a full day to get the meat moved to the river and loaded onto the boat. They had to hurry to break down the two camps so that Anthony could get back to school on the day that Ethan had promised Jonny that he would be back.

When they were pulling into Fort Yukon, a teenage friend of Anthony's saw the antlers in the boat. Within ten minutes, a dozen teenagers and the same number of adults came to the river to admire the trophy.

Anthony gave most of the meat to needy families that he knew in town. He saved the best cuts, though, for his uncle and himself to enjoy throughout the winter.

Ethan helped him hang the antlers on the wall under the porch roof. They hung next to some moose antlers that his dad had taken years before.

The antlers represented new life for a boy who had nearly taken his own there on that very porch. As the three men (for Anthony had become a man on that hunt) admired the moose antlers, all three felt hope for the future that those antlers represented.

Chapter 41

The next day, Ethan bid his friends in Fort Yukon farewell and promised to return as soon as the ice cleared, possibly even sooner if FSO had any clients who wanted an ice fishing adventure on the Yukon.

Jonny let Ethan use an old shed to store most of his camp gear. The boat was light for the trip down to the takeout.

It was a beautiful fall day. The breeze held a chill, forecasting the upcoming winter, but for now, the sun was providing just enough warmth to make the boat ride comfortable.

Though he was alone with his thoughts, the fall day felt like a familiar friend. He thought about all that had happened with Anthony. It seemed that being out in nature and being immersed in the adventure of hunting had shocked him out of his depression and apathy much like the shock of his arrow hitting that shotgun.

Ethan could relate. It wasn't that long ago when his mental and emotional health hung in the balance and the medicine of nature had healed him, bringing him back to life as well.

He arrived at his takeout and loaded the boat onto the trailer to take back to Fairbanks for the winter. Even as he worked and began the long drive south, his thoughts were with all the young native Alaskans who were as desperate for purpose and fulfillment in life as Anthony was.

He felt their desperation and wondered if there was anything that he could do to help. An idea hit him. Maybe he could start a summer outdoor adventure camp for kids who were high risk for suicide.

His mind raced with the possibilities and details and he couldn't wait until he could bounce the idea off of Cody. It would take a lot of planning and fundraising, but maybe FSO could add a camp to the trips and programs that they were already doing,

He checked his cell phone even though he knew he wouldn't get service until he was closer to Fairbanks. The idea that he could make a significant difference in other people's lives gave Ethan excitement for his own purpose and significance. Maybe this was the next step in his own healing as well. The thought of the possibility of a youth camp made the drive back go quickly.

Several hours later, his thoughts were interrupted with his phone going crazy. As he got back into cell service, what looked like a hundred texts all hit at once and it chimed for thirty seconds while they all loaded.

"I guess I've been away from my phone for a minute." He didn't like to have technology with him in the wilderness, so he had left his phone in the truck since his last trip to Fairbanks. He couldn't imagine who all these texts were from. He could look later, but for now, he needed to call Cody.

"Hello."

"Hey Cody, I have an…"

"Hey there, movie star!"

"What? What are you talking about?"

"Oh, you don't know? You're an internet sensation! Seems one of our clients has a bit of a following on social media. He posted a video of his hunt with you and the end of the video shows you shooting a shotgun out of Anthony's hands with your bow. The YouTube video has gone viral with millions of views in just a few weeks."

"Oh, great!" Ethan started scrolling through his texts. A few he saw were from friends and fellow guides, but a lot of them were news reporters, newspaper writers, bloggers, all wanting an exclusive interview with him.

"So Ethan, my phone's ringing off the hook with everyone looking for you. Some of them wanted your coordinates. I've been holding them at bay by being vague about where you are.

"I knew you and Anthony needed time to tear down the camps. How do you want to handle this? I don't think I can stall forever."

"Umm...I'm not sure. Let me get home and watch the video and then go through my texts. Maybe I can just do a blog or radio show or something here in Fairbanks. I don't really want my face all over the place. Thanks for covering for me, Cody. Hopefully, this will just die out.

"I do want to talk to you about an idea I have to help the native Alaskans, but I'll call you back when I get a handle on this."

"Sounds good. Talk to you soon, Ethan."

"Bye, Cody. Thanks again."

Ethan couldn't imagine what all the fuss was about. He stopped for groceries and then made his way home and plugged in his laptop. While he was waiting for it to charge, he looked more closely at his texts. Some of the reporters had texted multiple times with financial incentives increasing with each text.

"This is crazy!" he whispered to himself as he poured himself a bowl of cereal. Normally, cereal wasn't part of his diet, but it had looked good at the store as a change from the camp food diet he'd been on.

It didn't take long to find Joey's video on YouTube, the most watched videos coming up in the queue first. It was thirty-five minutes long, so he skipped ahead to the last part. Ethan hadn't realized that Joey had been filming him as they snuck up on Johnny's house. When Ethan had taken the shot, Joey had edited the video to show the flight of the arrow in slow motion, much the same as Ethan had remembered it happening during the actual shot. He watched again as the arrow arced up and then back down again, the feather fletching catching the sunlight with each rotation.

In the slow motion video, Ethan caught something that he hadn't seen when it happened live. Right at the apex of the arc, the arrow hit a tiny branch from a tree that he had failed to notice at the time. It diverted the arrow just slightly to the right causing it to smack the stock of the gun soundly.

He swiped back and then paused the video just before it struck the branch. It looked like the arrow would have hit about 2 inches to the left of the gun and probably would have hit the wall of the house if it hadn't been diverted by the branch.

Ethan shuddered and wondered. "What are the odds that I hit that branch perfectly to redirect the shot? What if I had missed?"

Chapter 42

The next week was a blur for Ethan as he was busy fielding questions about the incident in Fort Yukon. He did several phone interviews and one for a local radio station, but had managed to keep his face away from video cameras.

He didn't want people in town to treat him differently and really didn't relish being a celebrity. Joey's video had only shown him from the back and had blurred out Anthony and Jonny's faces to protect their privacy.

The reporters had asked about who the young man was, but Ethan had managed to protect Anthony's identity. He told them that he was doing well and had people in his life to help him succeed in the future. Most of the reporters were unhappy with that answer, but they soon saw his resolve to be vague and didn't press him further.

Ethan had about a dozen friends in Fairbanks who knew who he was by sight, but he asked them not to make a fuss over him and to not let strangers know who he was until all this could settle down and blow over.

Right now the whole thing was all hyped up, but he knew that internet fame was fickle and short-lived. There would soon be the next viral video to replace Joey's and he could go back to normal life.

After two days without a call, Ethan thought he was in the clear, but, at 6:00 in the morning on Saturday, an unknown number rang his phone. He let the call go through to voicemail and waited until after breakfast to listen.

"Hi Ethan, this is um…Margo Smith with the Denver Post. I've been sent up to Fairbanks to write a story on the video of the thwarted suicide attempt in Fort Yukon. I'm wondering if you could meet with me for about an hour. I'm calling from my hotel room here in Fairbanks. Please call back on this number at your convenience."

There was something familiar about the voice of this reporter, but there was a lot of background noise on the call so Ethan didn't think too much about it. He called her back and they set up a time and place to meet later that afternoon.

"So, I'm happy to do an interview, but please, no pictures or video. I like my privacy." The reporter promised to use just a voice recording for the interview.

Ethan then called Mark. "Hey, I've got to meet a reporter at The Banks at 1:00. Do you and Leah want to meet me there for lunch first? Then, if it's not going well, I can give you a signal and you guys can interrupt with an urgent phone call to get me out of there."

Mark laughed. "You're crazy, but yeah, we'll meet you for lunch and we can rescue you if need be. I think Ohio State plays today, so we'll just watch the game while you do your famous guy stuff."

"Thanks, Mark. I owe you one."

Mark laughed. "No. You're buying lunch. We're even."

"Deal!" Ethan again wondered how he had lucked out with friends like Mark and Leah so quickly up here in Alaska.

Before driving to the restaurant, he showered and shaved prior to meeting the reporter. He had done several interviews already, but he was still nervous to talk to news reporters.

After pizza, the three friends were enjoying a beer and watching the game on the big screen TV mounted behind the bar. Ethan had nearly forgotten about the interview, but winced when he heard "Ethan?" from a female voice behind him.

Mark and Leah both looked up and Ethan saw Mark point at him. He tipped the front of his cowboy hat down to shadow his face and slowly turned around in his seat to face the reporter.

Mark watched as the color drained from his friend's face when he saw the reporter who continued, "...or should I call you Jake?"

Leah stood up from her chair and asked, "Ethan, are you all right? Why did she call you Jake?"

Ethan didn't reply to Leah, but instead turned to the reporter. "Can we step outside?" he asked, starting for the door.

Ethan turned back for a brief look at his friends. Mark was holding up his phone with a questioning look on his face. Ethan held up a hand with a slight shake of his head and Mark set the phone back onto the table.

When they stepped outside, Ethan was relieved to find that all the other customers were inside watching the game. He led the way to a secluded table on the patio and sat down. They were both silent for about thirty seconds until Ethan broke the silence with a voice barely audible.

"How did you find me, Molly?"

Chapter 43

"No! You don't get to ask the questions. This is my interview, Jacob."

It had been so long since he had heard his real name, Jake had almost forgotten that's who he was. He had taken the name and identity of Ethan, had started over, and had not looked back.

Now, looking across the table at Molly, his heart raced. She was clearly mad, but to Jake, she had never looked more beautiful. Her hair was shorter. She always used to wear it long. It was curlier, with several loose strands framing her face.

Her eyes were intense with anger, but he could also see a glimmer of excitement in those eyes. His mind raced with questions, "Is she excited to see me? Why is she here? How did she find me? Does she still care about me? Could she ever love me again?"

That one look into her eyes inspired a few seconds of hope, but it was short-lived. When she crossed her arms, he caught a flash of light on her left hand, a wedding ring. His heart dropped and he braced himself for her questions.

"Why are you pretending to be someone else? How could you let me believe you were dead?" Jake went through possible replies in his head, but nothing sounded right, not even to him.

"I don't know what to say, M, but I think I can show you something that will help you understand. It's in my truck."

Molly followed Jake to his truck, as if, now that she had found him, she didn't trust that he wouldn't disappear again. He opened the passenger door and rummaged through a camo day pack on the seat until he found what he was looking for. He pulled out a leather-bound journal. When Molly saw it, she gasped. "The journal! After you...died, I looked all over for that. I told myself that if I found it, I could understand why you did it."

"I'm sorry, M. Here's what I wanted you to see." Jake pulled an envelope out of the journal. It was yellowed and wrinkled and simply said "Jake" on the front.

"I found this that morning. I was still groggy and hungover from the night before, but my scanner had woken me up. Listening to the radio traffic, I went outside the cabin to drive up to the park to see if I could help, but my Cruiser was gone, and I found this letter stuck in my door. I was able to piece it together after I read this." He handed Molly the envelope.

Molly sat down on the curb and opened the envelope to read the letter inside. She first looked to the end to see who the writer was. "Your friend, Ethan."

"Jake," it began. "Even though we have only just met, I have never known anyone with a kinder heart, and yet, you are still a man's man. You listened to my story and you genuinely cared. I have never had a better friend. I thank you for that.

"I wish that we had met earlier in life. My only regret is that our friendship was so short-lived.

"I know that you are looking for a fresh start and I also know that I am in my last days. What I say next is going to sound crazy, but hear me out.

"I want to go out on my own terms, not in a hospital bed, fighting until the end. I know you would try to stop me if I told you about my plan. I can't afford another seventy-two hour hold in the hospital because, by then, I may be too weak to pull this off, so this letter will be goodbye.

"If you want it, I'm offering you my identity for a fresh start. My wallet has my driver's license and my social security card in it. You can have access to my bank accounts, insurance, investment accounts, etc. My wallet, keys, and all the info you'll need is at my house on the kitchen counter. Take the house and the car. Use them or sell them as you want. You can have everything that was me; a total identity swap.

"By the time you read this, I will be gone. I'm taking a few things from your cabin and the back shed to make this look like it was you and then you can pull off the identity switch. Don't be sad for me. This is how I want to go. I'm so glad that I met you, Jake.

Your friend, Ethan.

P. S. Sorry about the Cruiser."

Chapter 44

Jake watched Molly's face as she read the letter. By the end, her eyes were wet with tears and her hand was over her mouth. When she finished reading, her eyes met his. Jake could see the questions in that look, so before she asked, he began.

"M, I wasn't doing well that week. After you told me you were dating Mike, I was extremely depressed. I went home and started drinking. I think that's why I didn't notice when Ethan started the cruiser early that morning. I was passed-out drunk.

After reading the letter, I walked over to Ethan's house. While I was there, I noticed several Grand county sheriff's cars headed into my cabin. I should have gone over and cleared things up right then, but I wasn't thinking straight, I was scared, and I hid out at Ethan's.

My mind was still reeling from losing you. I thought maybe the police would think that I murdered Ethan and then rigged the incident in the Park to make it look like my suicide. I thought it might seem like I would do that to get his money.

M, I swear, I haven't touched any of his stuff. I only used his house and car for a few months, but I haven't taken any of his money.

Molly nodded and smiled. "I believe you, Jacob. You always have had amazing integrity, even when we were kids." The vote of confidence from Molly warmed Jake in the cool fall air, but her smile melted him.

"How does she do that?" he thought. "She still kills me with that smile."

Jake continued, "As the weeks went by, I was shocked that they hadn't identified the body as Ethan's and then started looking for me. The house was stocked with so much food, so I didn't go out except to do my run in the middle of the night.

I guess I just allowed myself to become Ethan. In my mind, I did a complete identity swap with him. I knew who I was, but I willed myself to become him to escape my own life. In a few months, I almost totally forgot that I wasn't Ethan. I started to think of myself as him. Eventually, I became Ethan and I put myself into his story in my mind.

Finally, the food in the house ran out and I went hunting, both for meat and to clear my head. I went north and just kept going. I knew that you were moving on with your life and nobody in Grand County trusted me anymore, so I just left it all and started over as Ethan, figuring no one would miss Jake."

Molly shook her head. "Jacob, you should have seen who showed up for your memorial service. All the staff from the west side of Rocky, ambulance, fire, law enforcement, nearly our whole class from high school were there; hundreds, Jacob. You touched so many lives. There wasn't a dry eye there that day."

Jake was deeply moved thinking about all those people who had missed him. "Thanks, M. That means a lot. I didn't think anybody cared about me after I blew it at the football game."

Several minutes ticked by as Jake and Molly sat in silence, thinking their own thoughts. Jake finally broke the silence.

"Now, if you are done with your 'interview,' I have a few questions for you."

"Okay, shoot." They smiled at each other, both feeling like somehow, the last two years without seeing each other was just a bad dream and they were as at ease with each other as they were in high school.

"How in the world did you find me up here?"

"Well, somehow, I never believed that you were gone. I could still feel you. Everybody said I was crazy and that I should just move on."

Jake interjected, "Well, it looks like you have, somewhat," he said, glancing down to Molly's left hand. Molly's face showed confusion for several seconds until she realized that Jake was talking about her ring.

"Oh, this? I forgot I still had it on. No, it's not real. I just started wearing it to keep guys from flirting at work or asking me out."

"What about Mike?"

"Mike is married, but not to me. You remember Sarah from school? They're actually expecting their first. They're really great together. No, after you died, I realized that I was not in love with Mike. He was just a safe guy to be with while I figured things out, but I never lost my love for you."

Jake's hopes soared. He took Molly's hand and brought it to his lips. At that moment, Mark and Leah came looking for their friend. They popped out of the door and saw him kissing the reporter's hand. Jake laughed when he saw their confused looks.

"Mark and Leah, allow me to introduce you to my friend, Molly from Colorado. Molly, these two are the coolest dogsledding couple in Alaska.

And…I guess, I should reintroduce myself to you guys. My name is Jake." Now, he could see that his friends were really confused.

"I see I have some explaining to do, but not here. Could we come over to your house this afternoon? This story is going to take a minute." Jake looked at Molly. "Is that okay?" she nodded yes, still holding his hand.

Molly's heart and mind raced. She had hoped and prayed that her hunch had been correct. She had flown all the way here, hardly daring to wish for him to be alive, yet here he was. She didn't know whether to be mad at him or to be ecstatic that he was alive and that he still seemed to care for her.

Jake opened the passenger door on his truck, but Molly scooted into the middle of the bench seat. He got in and wrapped his arm around her shoulder like they used to drive.

Normally, Jake liked to drive with a manual transmission, but today he was glad that this truck was an automatic. He didn't want to use his right hand to shift or do anything but hold on to Molly.

She laid her head on his shoulder as they drove. Both had so many unanswered questions, but for now they were content to just enjoy each other's company. Molly placed her hand on Jake's chest to feel the heartbeat that she feared had stopped two years ago. She closed her eyes and inhaled deeply, smiling as she remembered what he smelled like.

Chapter 45

When they got to Mark and Leah's house, the couple was feeding their dogs, so Jake's story would have to wait. Molly immediately fell in love with the sled dogs and asked Leah question after question ranging from asking about each individual dog to what the races were like.

Jake and Mark stood off to the side and watched the girls greet and feed each dog. When they were out of earshot, Mark asked, "how come you never told us about Molly before, Ethan…I mean, Jake? Man, your new name is going to take some getting used to."

"Yeah…I guess that was a different lifetime for me. I wasn't expecting to ever go back. But then, here she is. I can't believe it! She just shows up out of the blue."

"Well, it's obvious you two are in love."

Jake blushed. "Yeah, I guess I never did have a good poker-face."

During dinner and for several hours after, Jake told his story, in even more detail than he had with Molly.

When he had finished, everyone was quiet until Mark spoke up. "How in the world did no one know you weren't Ethan and how did nobody figure out that the body wasn't you?"

Jake shrugged, "I know. I stayed out of sight until I was in Wyoming, but the identity of the body's a mystery to me too."

Molly spoke up. "I think I might know how it happened. Are you guys up for my side of the story now?"

"Yes, please!" Leah chimed in.

Mark added, "Sure. Why not? This is way better than the spy movie we were going to watch tonight."

Molly took in a deep breath and let it out with a sigh. Remembering what had happened brought back a flood of emotions and she glanced over at Jake before starting her story to assure herself that he was still actually there.

"When Jake died, I was devastated. Even though we were going through a rough time in our relationship, he was my whole world. When he was gone, I kinda fell apart. I had to take time off work because I kept making mistakes and I would often just break down and cry in front of patients."

"Oh, M, I'm so sorry. I had no idea."

"How could you, Jacob? You were 'dead'." She used air quotes when she said the word dead. Jake could feel a tinge of sarcasm and resentment in her voice, but her smile spoke a promise of forgiveness eventually, if not quite yet.

She continued, "I never got closure and didn't ever get to say goodbye because I never saw the body. I mourned Jacob's death, but couldn't shake the feeling that he wasn't actually really gone. I tried to convince myself that he had died, but it didn't work.

My friends, co-workers, family, everybody was saying to let him go, but I couldn't. My mind said he was dead but…" Molly looked over at Jake "...my soul said you were still here.

After about a month, the pain subsided a bit and I was able to get back to work, but the turmoil in my mind raged, constantly jumping from the logical thought of you being dead to the absurdity of hope that somehow you were still alive."

Molly was now just speaking to Jake, having forgotten that Mark and Leah were in the room. Their eyes were locked and the pain that Jake saw in Molly's caused him now to deeply regret following Ethan's plan.

Molly continued her story. "Nearly every morning when I woke up, I believed you were alive. My dreams of you were so vivid, so real." At this part of the story Molly choked up and she took several minutes to compose herself before continuing.

"So, this was how it went until just three weeks ago. A co-worker showed me a video on YouTube about this guy named Ethan up in Alaska shooting a shotgun out of the hands of a suicidal youth with an arrow.

"In the video I couldn't see your face, but I recognized the mannerisms, the way that you walked and even the way that you cant your bow slightly to the side when you shoot. It all seemed too familiar.

"I remembered that there had been an Ethan at the hospital at that time, so I went back and checked the records. The names matched up, but I still had a bunch of questions.

"Fortunately, I have a friend who works at the coroner's office. She wasn't supposed to, but she let me look at your file. After I saw that file, I booked a ticket to Fairbanks.

"I've actually been here for ten days. Turns out you're kind of a hard guy to track down. I made up the story about being a reporter so that you wouldn't run."

Leah's voice piped up, tense with excitement and intrigue. "What did you find in that file?" Molly smiled, now remembering Mark and Leah.

"That week, the county coroner was on vacation and his new assistant was on call for Grand County. The assistant was unfamiliar with how things were done and he made many mistakes on his first death investigation. He was supposed to do a thorough investigation of the body before he sent it to Denver for organ harvest, but he knew that time was of the essence to salvage the organs, so he sent it down by ambulance right away.

"The paperwork was all messed up. It said that the body had been identified, but the assistant made assumptions based on the vehicle, the uniform, and the wallet they found and he hadn't really positively identified the body.

"On the way down to Denver, the ambulance got caught behind a rock slide on Berthoud Pass. By the time the road was cleared and they got to the hospital, it was too late to harvest any organs. Since the paperwork stated that the investigation of the body had been completed, the hospital in Denver went ahead and had the body cremated.

"When the coroner finally returned home, there was no evidence for him to look at. Even the Cruiser had been towed away for parts and there wasn't a paper trail for him to track it down. He amended the report, noted the obvious discrepancies, and fired the assistant.

"He did make a note in the report that there was no evidence pointing to the body being any other than Jacob's and that there were witnesses in town who observed him that day in obvious distress and driving recklessly. He said in the report that he believed that it was Jacob.

"The report was not conclusive that the body wasn't Jake's, but it gave me some hope. The report, the video, and my own gut feeling told me that I had to know for sure. I had to find where this Ethan was to see if he could possibly be my Jacob.

"Honestly, I was thinking that it would probably turn out to be Ethan, his liver making a miraculous recovery, and I could finally move on." She flashed Jake another soul-melting smile. "I'm so glad I was wrong."

Jake drove Molly back to her hotel in Fairbanks and walked her to her door. "I'm glad you're not dead, Jacob. I can see now why you did it."

"Thanks, M. That means a lot. I'm also glad I'm not dead." They laughed and Molly pointed her thumb at the door.

"You want to come in?"

Jake paused for several seconds before replying. "No. There's a line in a country song that says 'just a kiss good night.' I think I've made a lot of mistakes with you, M. Tonight, I don't want to mess this thing up, so I'm content with just a kiss goodnight. Is that okay?"

After a long kiss, Jake's hand remained around the side of Molly's neck and he looked deeply into her eyes. "You said earlier that you never stopped loving me. You need to know that I didn't either. Even when I thought you had moved on, I couldn't. For me, no other girl could replace you, M."

After one more kiss, he said, "I love you, M. Thanks for finding me. See you tomorrow."

Molly's emotions wouldn't let her speak, so she stepped backwards into her room and slowly shut the door. She immediately looked through the peep hole to watch Jake for as long as possible, still not quite believing that this was real.

Chapter 46

Over the next several days, Jake and Molly caught up on the last two years of their lives while exploring the area around Fairbanks. Molly was used to the Shiras moose in Colorado, but was amazed when she saw her first Alaska/Yukon bull moose. Its sheer body size and massive antlers dwarfed its southern cousin.

Leah took the two out on a wheeled dog sled to give Molly the full Alaskan cultural experience. She packed a lunch for them to enjoy on the trail. They spread out a blanket and enjoyed the last days of an Indian summer. The October sun was warm enough that they were comfortable with light jackets, but the chill of the breeze told of the change of the season that would soon come to the northlands.

Leah left them alone to take care of the dogs and Jake used the opportunity to ask Molly some burning questions. "Hey, M, I guess you'll need to be getting back to work, huh?"

Molly smiled and teased, "Trying to get rid of me so soon?"

Jake squeezed her hand. "Never. I just know how much your job means to you."

"I do love what I do, but the good thing about nursing is that you can get a job anywhere."

Jake's heart raced, not daring to hope for what he thought Molly was saying. "So, you could work in, say…Milwaukee?"

"Yes, I guess Milwaukee would be an option…" The seconds ticked by, both hoping the other's feelings were as strong as their own. "…but recently, I've been thinking about working at a hospital in

Fairbanks, providing that the other living conditions up here meet my approval."

With that, Jake was sure of her feelings and he pulled her to him and kissed her. He then pulled back slightly to look into her eyes. "Are you sure?"

A few seconds ticked by before Molly answered. "Jacob, I lost you once and it nearly killed me. I'm sure!"

They kissed again, a long, drawn-out kiss that seemed to melt away all of their questions. This time, Molly pulled back.

"...but, I didn't come up here to be with Ethan. I want you to be Jacob again."

Jake paused, wondering what would happen if he went to the authorities with his secret. Would he be charged with some kind of identity theft? Would there be jail time? What about a criminal record, and how would that affect his work?

"Any other conditions?"

"Yes, I loved your beard. Can you grow that back?"

"Fair enough. If you're willing to relocate to Alaska in return for me changing my name back and growing a beard, I think we have a deal. Shake on it?" Jake said, extending his hand toward her.

Molly slapped away his hand. "Shut up, you idiot. Let's kiss on it." She tackled him onto his back and they did just that.

That afternoon, Jake made good on his promise. He first called Cody and told him the whole story. "Well, Jake, I knew there was probably more to your story and how you came to be alone in the wilderness when we found you out there. Thanks for telling me."

"Cody, I don't know how this is going to go down. You might need to find somebody else who can run things up here if I end up in jail."

"Nope. You're my man, Jake. It'll work out fine." Once again, Cody seemed to know things about Jake that he didn't know about himself. He wished he had Cody's optimism.

He next drove to the police station in Fairbanks and told them his story. They charged him with identity theft, set a court date, and released him, since he had turned himself in and volunteered the information.

His hearing happened the week before Thanksgiving. After the judge and district attorney reviewed all the information, they found that Jake hadn't spent any of the money, and had only used a deceased man's identity without financial benefit to himself.

They decided that, not only would the charges of identity theft be dropped, but thought that the letter that Ethan wrote before he died, if authenticated, could act as a last will and testament. The judge advised Jake to hire an attorney to transfer Ethan's assets to him, as it seemed clear from the letter that he wanted Jake to have those assets.

Jake was blown away. Not only was he not being punished, he was possibly going to be rewarded financially from this whole thing. Jake, Molly, Mark, and Leah met at *The Banks* after the hearing to celebrate.

After ordering his food, Jake stepped outside to call Cody and told him the good news.

"I told you it would all turn out okay. I think you've got someone looking out for you. Probably, the Good Lord is collaborating with your parents up there to pull some strings." They both laughed, but Jake wondered and was amazed at the thought.

"Hey Cody, I'm also going to need some advice from you pretty soon, I mean, marriage and family advice."

"Wow! Congrats, Jake. That's awesome! I'm really happy for you. Jillian will be thrilled."

Thanksgiving Day was cold and snowy. Jake and Molly met at Mark and Leah's for a huge feast. The dogs were even allowed to eat some turkey for the special day. Jake was incredibly thankful as he thought about his life. He thought about how crazy it was that a video on the internet of him shooting an arrow had brought Molly back to him.

He looked at her across the table as she and Leah were talking and laughing. They were well on their way to being as good of friends as he and Mark had become.

It looked like he might be able to use Ethan's money to start his summer youth camp up on the Yukon. He was extremely excited to get that going.

Molly had applied for and immediately been offered a job at the hospital in Fairbanks starting in January. She had asked for part of the summer off to help with the camp. It looked like they were willing to work with her on that and have a temporary nurse fill in for the summer. On this day, Jake was incredibly thankful.

After everyone was finished eating, he asked if he could read something. He pulled out his old journal with the original notepad that was in it when Molly had given it to him in middle school. He read the first entry for everyone.

"A girl gave me this. She said it would help me. I don't know, but I guess I'll give it a try. I don't know what to write, so I guess I'll write about her. She's really pretty. I like her hair and she runs really fast, faster than some of the boys. The best thing about her is her smile. I need that. Her smile is like Mom's. She calls me Jacob, like Mom did. I want to be her friend, maybe forever."

The next afternoon, Jake took Molly to Chena Hot springs. They waded into the hot pool after it got dark. The steam from the springs obstructed their view at times, but when the wind would clear it away, they could see the Northern Lights dancing overhead, a first for Molly.

She was entranced by the spectacle, but Jake couldn't watch the lights. He was too absorbed watching that captivating smile dance across her face while the lights danced across the sky.

Sitting in the hot water with their hair frozen from the cold air, he gave her the ring that he had had kept with him all these years, bought before he had broken his leg. He asked if she would be his friend forever.

Author note:

This story contains many references to suicide and suicidal thoughts. I didn't set out to write a book about suicide, but it kind of just wrote itself into the story.
If you regularly experience suicidal thoughts, please seek help from a counselor, pastor, or trusted friend.
I believe that you can find lasting hope for your life. I encourage you to choose the harder path and find purpose for your life that will positively affect both yourself and others.

About the author

Doug Treat grew up on a farm in Kansas where he learned how to work hard and be resourceful. Through different seasons in his life, he has worked as a carpenter, security officer, EMT, and a plethora of other endeavors and experiences that have found their way into this story.

For several decades, he lived within a few miles of Rocky Mountain National Park in Colorado. He has hiked and backpacked extensively in the area.

He has bowhunted since he was fourteen years old and believes that the ultimate adventure involves backpacking and bowhunting with a bit of backcountry fishing and photography thrown in for good measure.

Doug now lives in Northern California. This is his first adventure as the author of a book.